WHEN MY HEART WAS WICKED

WHEN MY HEART WAS WICKED

TRICIA STIRLING

SCHOLASTIC PRESS
NEW YORK

All rights reserved. Published by Scholastic Press, an imprint of Scholastic Inc., *Publishers since 1920*. SCHOLASTIC, SCHOLASTIC PRESS, and associated logos are trademarks and/or registered trademarks of Scholastic Inc.

Library of Congress Cataloging-in-Publication Data

Stirling, Tricia, author.
When my heart was wicked / Tricia Stirling. — First edition.
    pages cm
    Summary: After her father dies, leaving sixteen-year-old Lacy with her much-loved stepmother, Lacy's birth mother suddenly shows up wanting Lacy back — and she will stop at nothing, not even dark magic, to control her daughter and draw her into her own twisted life.
    ISBN 0-545-69573-2 — ISBN 978-0-545-69573-2 1. Mothers and daughters — Juvenile fiction. 2. Stepmothers — Juvenile fiction. 3. Magic — Juvenile fiction. 4. Choice (Psychology) — Juvenile fiction. [1. Mothers and daughters — Fiction. 2. Stepmothers — Fiction. 3. Magic — Fiction. 4. Choice — Fiction.] I. Title.
    PZ7.1.S75Wh 2015
    813.6 — dc23
                                                                                    2014021741

10 9 8 7 6 5 4 3 2 1   15 16 17 18 19

Printed in the U.S.A.   23
First edition, March 2015

Book design by Jeannine Riske

To Shane. My heart is yours, always.

CHAPTER ONE

My stepmother, Anna, swears magic exists in the everyday. I used to think she was full of it, but then one morning at Big Chico Creek we found a mermaid's eye under a patch of bird's-foot trefoil. The eye was large and perfectly round like a human's, but it had the glittering green iris of a fish. After that, I started noticing magic in other places too. A swan serenading a catfish at Horseshoe Lake, her neck arching like a quivering bow in song. A boy with the legs of a goat, playing the flute from his canoe along the river.

Since my dad died, though, I haven't spotted a single bit of magic. Not even a shooting star, or the quiet unfurling of a fiddlehead fern frond at dawn.

⁜

Anna spoons vegetarian chili onto her tofu dog. The spoon makes a clattering noise against the blue chili bowl. "Are you sure you're ready to go back, Lacy? I know you miss your friends and the routine and all that, but we could keep homeschooling until summer; you can start as a senior in the fall." She reaches for the pitcher of water garnished with floating bits of mint and slices of lemon from our garden. "Besides, I'll miss having you around."

I take a bite of my own tofu dog, which I still maintain tastes like weird cheese, and shake my head. True, Shell and Mechelle think I'm crazy to want to go back to school, but they don't understand. They don't know what it's like here all day, in this sad house, where Anna and I tiptoe around each other in grief. Like ballerinas in some tragedy, we move so quietly, careful not to touch each other, as though the slightest contact might send us spinning off the stage.

Since my dad has been gone, dinner is often a silence so loud it makes my ears ring. To mask it, Anna sometimes plays the Grateful Dead or some other hippie music from a million years ago, from a time before Anna was even born. While the music plays, we think of things to say to each other in the spaces between the songs. Anna is one of the nicest people I've ever known, and the truth is, she never asked for this — a teenager to raise on her own. We just don't always know what to say to each other, so we talk around the silences, we talk around his empty chair.

"I want to go back," I say carefully, as though what I'm saying could somehow be taken wrong. "I miss everyone. I miss being busy."

Anna glances at her knitting basket on the kitchen counter, heaped with skeins of thick orange wool, and smiles because she gets it. She knits to keep her hands busy. She knits because it keeps her mind off things. She's always knitted, but never like this. It has been a hard four months, but we are rich in knitted sweaters.

"Shell said there's a new science club meeting on Wednesdays after school. We're going to join together."

"What about Mechelle?"

"No. She hates science. She's going out for the spring musical, anyway."

Anna smiles. "That I can see." She laughs. She's probably thinking about the time in eighth grade when my friends and I put on a play in the backyard. Mechelle wore tap shoes and a sequined leotard, a feather boa, and face paint like a cat. She sang "Memory" while the neighbor's dog howled, and her dark skin glistened in the sun and she looked more like an angel than a cat on the ugly makeshift stage. Shell and I stammered through our lines, embarrassed and laughing. We would rather dissect flowers than go out for the spring musical. But then, we'd rather dissect flowers than do most things.

"Will you need a ride?" Anna asks.

"No," I say, but then I imagine myself arriving alone to my first day of school in four months. I imagine everyone staring at me as I walk up to the front doors, thinking, *Poor Lacy, poor little orphan girl; first her mother left her, and now she's lost her dad.* So I say, "I don't know. Maybe."

⁜

Anna drives a sky-blue 1971 Volkswagen bus. You can hear us coming from a block away, I know. When we pull up to school, kids stare. They all arrive in Toyota Priuses and Camrys, normal cars that don't make a sound. But I love our blue Volkswagen. We've slept in it and cooked in it. We've taken it across America. Anna says it's mine when I get my license. "It's time for me to settle down, get a sensible vehicle," she says. But I can't see her driving anything else.

Shell comes running up, her hair, which she has recently dyed magenta, bouncing and shining with streaks of gold in the sun.

"Hey," she says, and she flashes a smile at Anna. I jump out of the bus. "Welcome back, Lacy," Shell says, but she rolls her eyes because she thinks I'm so crazy to want to be here. Already, though, school feels like normal to me, like cheese dogs and science lab, not frozen veggie casseroles we'll defrost and put on our plates but not eat, not layers of dust on the neck of my dad's guitar.

"Hi, Shell. Bye, Anna," I say, rolling the window back up. You can't open the passenger seat door from the inside, so you have to roll down the window and stick your arm out to access the handle on the outside of the door. "Thanks for the ride."

"My pleasure," Anna says. "Good luck."

I link arms with Shell and we head inside.

⁂

We push open the glass double doors, and in a whoosh, the stale air from the heater pumps into my face. The halls are still pretty empty, but they won't be for long. I hear footsteps on the linoleum, a slamming locker, a high-pitched giggle like a joke or imitation. My heart starts to pound and my palms sweat. I wipe them on my jeans. Just like that, I'm not sure exactly how I thought this would feel like normal.

The last time I was here, my father was alive and I was just like everyone else. My mom had left, but so what; moms leave. Now, though, everything's different, and maybe everyone will treat me weird. Maybe no one will know what to say, so they won't say anything at all. Shell walks close beside me so our arms touch. I pretend the friction from our arm hairs is a force field no one can penetrate.

Then Mechelle and some of her theater friends round the corner, and when she sees me, Mechelle tilts her head and opens her arms and hugs me, and her friend Todd throws his arms around us both and kind of jumps up and down. And everyone around us is laughing and talking and no one is treating me different at all. Some girl I only know by sight offers me a piece of gum, and I take it. When Zach comes around the corner and sees me, he grins his funny gap-toothed grin and punches me in the gut, so I'll know he's not feeling sorry for me. It's a very light punch, but I know what he's doing: letting me know I'm still just weird old Lacy to him, the girl who prefers cataloguing plants to ordering clothes from catalogues. I punch him back, just a tiny bit harder, so he'll know he doesn't have to be delicate with me.

"Hey, Science Freak," he says. "Chemistry hasn't been the same since you left. There's no one smarter than Mr. Ramsy anymore, so he can say anything and we have no choice but to believe him. I think even he misses you correcting him every few minutes."

"I don't correct him every few minutes!"

"Once a day at least."

"Well, yeah."

"He almost got in trouble the other day. Abram tried correcting him on something, and Mr. Ramsy goes 'Can I call you Camel Jockey?'"

"Are you serious?" I throw my extra books into my locker, and we start walking together to class.

"Yeah, but Abram was just like 'Can I call you Imperialistic Pig?' And everyone laughed and it was over."

"He probably could have gotten fired for that."

"I know. He probably should've. He's such a racist."

"I know, and he doesn't know anything about chemistry, either."

I say that, and it's true that Mr. Ramsy gets a lot of his facts mixed up. It's also true that we have a boy named Tuong in the class, and Mr. Ramsy is always telling this totally unfunny joke where Tuong's parents drop a fork on the ground and decide to name their kid whatever sound the fork makes. He'd already told that joke at least ten times before I left to homeschool. He's kind of a jerk, but none of us takes him too seriously and I don't think he means any harm really. He's kind of just not very smart. And the fact is, in spite of Mr. Ramsy, I absolutely love chemistry. I even just love being inside the classroom, with its huge periodic table and the lab stations and Bunsen burners. I can almost pretend I'm a real scientist when I'm in there.

Zach and I are almost to class now and I wish I could slow down and we could keep talking, but it's too late. We part as soon as we get inside the door.

"See you after class," Zach says, and he goes to his seat at the back of the room. I take my old seat near the front next to Mechelle, and she pinches me and I smile. She and Shell are the only ones who know that I like Zach, that I have ever since we had to do an oral report together as our final last year in French. We could choose any topic we wanted, and he wanted to do Anne Frank. I think I wanted to do the report on French cheese or something. Anne Frank was a much cooler idea, and he was so sweet about the whole thing. I think he may have been a tiny bit in love with Anne, which is probably why I fell a tiny bit in love with him. Sometimes I think he likes me back. But so far, neither of us has made a move. I'm waiting for him to do it. I'd be mortified if I let him know I liked him that way and it turned out it was all in my head. He'd be like, "Let's be friends," and I'd die.

We spend the period identifying isotopes. I think it's so cool how, in chemistry, everything is a symbol for something else. The old alchemical symbol for gold looks like a punk rock eyeball or a baby bird. Everything fits together and you get to wade through this amazing microscopic world of atoms and molecules to solve the ancient riddles, and everything has an answer. Alchemy — turning base metals to gold, the transformation of something ordinary into something extraordinary. One bucketful of water contains more atoms than there are bucketsful of water in the Atlantic Ocean. It's just like magic. Diamond and graphite are both pure carbon. If that is true, then anything is possible. For a whole hour, I don't think once about my father. When the bell rings, it's like having to leave Wonderland.

Second-period algebra sludges by, with Mr. Garcia talking about probability and statistics, but in French we get to watch an old TV show called *Le Professeur* and in English we get to write haiku. I write about last summer: We climbed to the top / of Monkey Face in August / bright Perseid sky. At lunch, Zach is waiting for me at my locker.

"Eat with me?" he asks.

"Sure." I smile apologetically at Shell and Mechelle, and they raise their eyebrows and purse their lips and smile.

I order pepperoni pizza for lunch, and we take our lunches to the quad where we sit on the grass against a wall. I take a bite of my pizza. It is greasy and delicious after four months of vegetarian health food.

"So I've kind of gotten behind in chemistry," Zach tells me. "My mom's pissed. She wants me to get a tutor."

"Oh." I put my pizza down on the grass. "Well, I could help you."

"Really? Like maybe I could come to your house a couple afternoons a week and you could help me catch up?"

"Sure," I say. "That would be great. I mean, that will be fun."

"Awesome. Thanks, Lacy."

"My pleasure." We smile at each other. I take a bite of my pizza, but I can't even taste it anymore. After the bell rings, I float through the rest of my day. Gym isn't as dreadful as usual because we are doing a unit on Tai Chi. My friends and I laugh all the way through it, making rainbows with our hands. It is good. It is good to be back.

⁜

I take the long way home from school so I can walk along the creek. The blackberries are blooming and will be ready to eat in a month. The invasive periwinkle blooms too, its purple flowers like the spring sky at night. Over two hundred years ago, the Maidu Indians lived right here along this creek in their houses made of bark. I think about them, the Maidu, and how much they knew about the natural world. Soap plant and sweet Indian potatoes, deer grass and yerba santa. They were immune to poison oak, so they cooked their bread in the leaves and wove the branches of the poison oak into baskets. I wish I knew everything there was to know about plants. I know a lot, but there are so many secrets I have still to uncover. I've read a ton of books, but I wish a real live Maidu woman would come out of the bushes and teach me. We'd weave a basket to carry sorrow for all the old ways that are

8

gone, and then another one to carry hope. I smile at the thought —
a beautifully woven hope basket.

When I'm almost home, I leave the creek and cross to the edge
of the park. White blossoms from the cherry trees whip through
the air like snow. Across the street, I can see Anna's blond hair
blowing like streaks of lightning across the sky — she is gardening in spite of the wind. I cross the street and she stands, brushing
dirt from her overalls.

"Hey, Lace," she says, shaking out her hands. "How was the
first day back?"

"Great. I'm going to start tutoring someone, okay? My friend
Zach. I guess he's gotten behind in chemistry. Is it okay if he
starts coming over after school?"

"After school?"

"Yeah. Just a couple times a week." I don't wait for her to answer.
I know Anna won't mind. I drop my backpack and kneel to pick
up my kitty cat, Mr. Murm. "Hey, Mr. Mr." I nuzzle my nose in
his fur, but he leaps from my arms. "What's with him? He seems
spooked."

Anna watches Mr. Murm as he dashes around the side of the
house, into the backyard.

I pluck a peapod from the vine and split it with my fingernail.
I always eat the whole thing, but in sections — skin first.

"The butter lettuce is looking really good. Do you want me to
harvest some for tonight's dinner?" She usually asks me to prepare
a side dish, something from the garden. I pop the peas single file
into my mouth.

"I thought we'd go out for dinner," Anna says, not quite meeting my eyes.

"What's wrong?"

"We should go inside," she says, and I notice the quick dart of her eyes. Suddenly the wind stills, and yet I feel an even sharper chill: Something is wrong; there's something dangerous in the air. I head up the steps to the porch, trying to figure it out. But it isn't until I get inside the house and smell her perfume that I realize what it is. My real mother, Cheyenne, has come back.

The smell of perfume (Bad Apple by Marie-Andre Bourdieu) mingles with the incense Anna is burning and I retch. Anna follows me inside and coughs.

"I'm sorry," she says. "I thought the incense would mask the smell."

The air in the living room even tastes like my mother. I feel like she's back inside me already, her taste in my mouth, her smell all around us. I walk into the kitchen and pour myself a glass of iced tea. "What did she want?" I ask, stones in my stomach.

Anna reaches behind herself and grasps the counter with both hands. "Well," she says. "She wants you."

CHAPTER TWO

Upstairs in my room, I cast a spell for protection. It's not that I think I'm a witch or anything. Or maybe I do. I don't know. Once I didn't think magic and science could go hand in hand, but now I absolutely think they can. That's what the Native Americans believed.

There was a time when I turned my back completely on the possibility of magic. That's why I didn't believe it when Anna swore it was out there. When I was little, my mother and I would go out at night and set incantations on fire. While the world slept, we'd toss curses into the flames. I thought it was pretend, a game we played, and maybe it was. But it was a scary game.

It is a fact that herbs can heal. People have studied this and proven it and written about it in science journals. Our ancestors relied on herbs for their healing properties. Later, they were burned at the stake as witches because the herbs had made them such powerful healers, and that was a threat to the old white guys who were in charge.

I'm a gardener and an herbalist, and I'm going to be an herbalist when I grow up. "I happen to dig botany," as the girl said in *Alice's Restaurant*, an old movie I watched with Anna and my dad. I have been studying plants and their medicinal properties since I came to live here in Chico three years ago. But even after rejecting the notion of magic because of my mom, the casting of spells is the one thing from my past I haven't completely let go of: herbal lore and the lighting of candles are so beautiful and steeped in tradition. And now I believe magic — good magic — and science can work side by side. Because living with Anna, I have seen that they both are real.

I remember when Anna got me my first book on herbalism. It was old and dog-eared and marked with notes in pencil. She got it for me at this used bookstore we have in town. It's called the Bookstore and it's crammed with stacks and piles of books. After that first book, we started going there together regularly to buy more books on herbs and plants.

"It's good to be armed with information," Anna liked to say. "The more you know, the more power you have over your own life."

My bedroom shelves are crammed with these books and bottles of herbs I've dried and tinctures I've made, and also candles I'm not allowed to burn. When I do cast spells, they are always for good, like now. A protection spell never hurt anyone. I gather up my glass jars of dill, St. John's wort, and vervain. I wrap the herbs in a swath of red fabric and hang them with black ribbon from the curtain rod above my window. And as I do so, I catch a glimpse of a dark-haired woman in the garden. I gasp, and she is gone.

⁜

When I moved in with my dad and Anna three years ago, I was a different girl. Hard and scared, with chopped-off hair and black eyeliner. I wore a bomber jacket even in the summer. I'd stolen it from a park bench while its owner played on the grass with his little kid, and with it on, I felt like I was invisible.

My dad and Anna planted me a moon garden of angel's trumpets, white roses, and larkspur and cosmos. The flowers climbed a series of posts like a teepee, and I'd sit beneath the garden at night. Once my eyes had adjusted to the dark, the flowers would seem to glow and float like pale lightning bugs in the sky. The world finally felt like it was beginning to slow down. I remembered how to breathe.

❖

The wind picks up throughout the afternoon and into the evening. I go outside to sprinkle dried angelica around the four corners of our property for additional protection, but the herbs scatter in the wind and blow away almost immediately. It doesn't matter. I wouldn't feel safe from my mother if we lived behind castle walls woven through with protection herbs and spells, behind a moat filled with deadly alligators. She'd find her way in. She always does.

I sit at my desk and attempt to do word problems. At least I know that soon Anna will take me out for dinner, and then I'll be able to breathe without hyperventilating, even if only for an hour or so. Here at home I can feel my mother's energy rolling like a toxic fog through the rooms. The smell of her perfume has infiltrated the cracks in the walls. I feel her everywhere. I can't seem to catch my breath.

I'm still on word problem number one when Anna taps with her fingertips on my open door.

"Are you about ready?" she asks.

"Let's go," I say. I don't even bother to close my book. I leap up and grab a sweatshirt, and then we're downstairs and out the door.

We walk downtown past some of my favorite places. The Senator Theater is a venue for concerts now, but in the old days it was a vaudeville house, with jugglers and animals and acrobats. At Ital Imports and Melody Records, you can buy actual records along with jewelry from Thailand, and incense and clothing from India and Guatemala. Jack's is open twenty-four hours and the waitresses call you hon. When my dad would let me, I used to go late with my friends and we'd listen to the drunk college kids, who talked about nothing but how totally wasted they were.

At the Bear, we order our food, then sit at our favorite table next to the Harry Potter pinball machine. "The Bear" is short for Madison Bear Garden, but no one calls it that. It's like a big junk-yard of wonderful things — the walls and ceilings are covered with old pictures and license plates and mechanical gadgetry like wheels and cogs and even full-size carriages from the olden days. Surfboards, torpedoes, a kayak. Anna says the door to the girls' bathroom used to say MEN and the boys' bathroom said WOMEN, only they each had a hand pointing to the other bathroom, and people would get confused and walk into the wrong room. But the signs aren't like that anymore.

To keep our minds off my mother, we are reading the funny fake ads on the menu. RAISE MOOSE IN YOUR BASEMENT says one ad, and Anna says, "We could hang our garden tools from the antlers." Another ad for some kind of spyglasses says SEE YOUR NEIGHBOR NAKED CLOSE UP. We just eye each other. Bald and weird-eyed Mrs. Jouve? No, thanks. We're sitting side by side, even though ordinarily we'd sit opposite each other. I know it's silly, but I want to feel safely ensconced in my booth, where no one can snatch me up and take me away. Anna on one side of me, and on the other, a wall of protection: old yearbook rugby pictures of boys with strong arms and ghostly faces. A man's voice booms from the loudspeaker, "Anna, come and get it. Your order's ready, Anna!"

"Do you want to come get it with me?" Anna asks, and even though I do, I shake my head. I'm not a child.

Still, when she comes back with our food — cheese fries and a Caesar salad for her, a Bear burger with curly fries for me — I am relieved to have her weight beside me. I feel light and insubstantial, like the kids in the old Shel Silverstein poem who get snatched up by gypsies and carried off in pillowcases. I inhale everything on my plate. While I eat, I imagine myself growing heavier, like a great tree with giant roots. I cannot be moved. I cannot be carried away. I suck at my Coke until the liquid is all gone and I'm sucking on air. Anna watches me, holding a cheese fry dripping with cheese.

"What?" I ask.

"You were hungry," she says.

"I'm scared," I admit, and she sighs.

"I know."

From somewhere in the restaurant, a child starts to scream. The sound is so shrill the windows might break. The glass might come raining down on the Harry Potter pinball machine and pierce our skin. I flinch and brush my ear with my hand, as if that might push the sound away.

"Tell me what she said," I say.

Anna takes a sip of her iced tea. "Are you sure you want to know?"

"It's my life. I want to know." I don't mean to be rude to Anna, but sometimes I can't help it. She thinks she can protect me from everything, but we learned when my dad died that isn't true. She couldn't protect me from that. She couldn't protect me from the nightmares that followed, from the loneliness and regret for all the times I was a bad daughter to him. And she can't protect me now. We both know it.

"She says she's been talking with her attorney. She's on parole. And she swears she's turned her life around. She heard about your dad." Anna looks up and I bite the side of my lip. These are the things we do to keep from crying: I bite my lip, she looks up. "And now she wants you to go live with her. She has a new place." I try to swallow, but my throat is dry. My heart might burst from my chest and fly away.

"Where?"

"Sacramento."

The stones in my stomach rumble and rise to my throat. Sacramento is where I've always lived with my mother. It's where we lived before she left. I close my eyes, and when I do, I envision them strung out before me: apartment after apartment and the occasional hotel room, each one as dumpy and dingy as the one before it. I see the ugly sprawling city in which I was always lost. I remember empty streets, crumpled paper blowing past the feet of junkies and homeless people. Once when I was little, a homeless man picked me up and tried to put me in his shopping cart, but I screamed and kicked him in the stomach and he let me go. Where was my mother? The apartment building we stayed the longest in was always hot and it had a sweet smell like orange juice, which sounds nice but it was horrible and rancid. My mother wouldn't give me a key to the apartment, so after school I'd have to stay at the park until dark, or sit under the stairs and trade bottle caps from my collection with the little boy in the building who was always trying to hide from his father.

· "But I don't want to go. I want to stay here and live with you."

"I want that too, honey, I really do. But legally I have no recourse. She's your mother. I'm just . . ." She's just the stepmom, but she doesn't say it. Instead, she holds her palms open before her in the air. They are empty. She is nothing.

"What about what I want? Doesn't the law care about that?"

Anna doesn't answer. We have both been through enough by now to know that it does not.

Across the room, a child's good mother calmly quiets its cries. Her soothing voice only makes me cry harder.

⁜

The trees are dark outside my bedroom window, but the moon lights the sky like a backdrop, and the trees teeter and seem to toast each other like people from a movie cocktail party. Anna's wind chimes bang against one another hard, and the sound is low and empty. Maybe it's drama to say they have an ominous tone, but my mood is already black and swirly like a night sky behind a castle in some other movie, one in which someone's about to go mad. Maybe the house will fly away and I'll land in a parallel universe, a time and place where my mother is happy and normal.

In real life, she's probably out there, out in this cold dark night. Spying on us once again. Watching through our windows.

Waiting. Counting down. It is warm inside my room, but I shiver uncontrollably, huddled beneath my blankets. Mr. Murm purrs softly.

I don't want to leave Anna. She's the only person alive who loves me. She's been married to my dad since I was seven, but they started dating when I was four. Up until three years ago, my primary residence was with my mom, but I'd come to Chico every other weekend and half of the summer. Anna is the one who held me on nights when I was in second grade and my mother didn't come to pick me up from school, didn't show up at all until eventually the school called my dad, who came to get me. He took me to his house and drove me back to school seventy miles each morning for a week until she suddenly reappeared. Anna is the one who helped me with my nightmares, teaching me to imagine myself a conqueror, to imagine the bad guys in goofy underwear and big clown shoes. After my dad died, she let me sleep in her bed with her for six nights until I told her I was ready to sleep alone. In spite of her own grief, she made me soup and hot chocolate, she knitted me a blanket and let me stay home from school for as long as I needed. She has become my home.

And Chico is my home now too. I don't want to leave Chico. It is the only town I've loved. I love the underwater caverns and tunnels at Bear Hole and the creek-fed swimming hole at Lower Bidwell Park. I love the oak trees and the stray cats who lie around in the sun, and outdoor Shakespeare in the summer, and the old Maidu Indian cave with the acorn-grinding pits carved into the rocks. It is springtime here, and the Thursday Night Farmers Market just started a couple of weeks ago. Anna and I have plans to get hennaed there; we have plans to go every Thursday. It was there last year that I found tiny little Mr. Murm sitting in a cardboard box and murming his sweet little song: *"Please take me home."*

In her room, Anna is watching a movie on her computer. I can hear occasional swells of heartbreaking music. I long to go in there, to curl up beside her on her bed, snuggle beneath the sheets, let her tell me the old stories of princesses and dragons, ones where evil lurks and strikes out, and good always wins in the end. But I don't want my mother to see me choose Anna over her on this dark night. She'll be angry.

She is still out there. I know it.

⁘

At school I am a wreck. Even chemistry fails to comfort me. I can't concentrate, and when Mr. Ramsey asks me a question, I can't answer because I don't know the answer and I didn't hear the question. I avoid Zach. I drop my books in the hallway and spill chocolate milk on my shirt.

"Are you okay?" Mechelle asks after second period. I'm a mess. I know I'm a mess.

"I don't think I'm going to be able to tutor Zach," I say, as though that is the only thing that matters. "If I'm not at school tomorrow, tell him to ask Shell to help him. Okay? Can you tell him that?"

"Dude, you're being cryptic. What's going on?"

"My mom came to my house yesterday. She wants me to move back to Sacramento with her."

"Oh no." Mechelle moves closer and puts her arm around me. I can't stand it. I can't stand people being nice to me right now.

19

I spin away and wait in the bathroom until the halls are clear. I'll get a late mark from Madame Sussman, but I don't care.

If Cheyenne lets me stay with Anna, I will happily do whatever busywork Mr. Garcia wants me to do. I will solve three hundred algebraic equations every night. I will wash his dry-erase boards with my tongue. I will be a perfect stepdaughter and never make Anna wish she hadn't ended up with me. I'll do anything. Just let me stay with Anna. Just please, please don't make me go live with my mother.

⁂

After school, she is waiting for me by the drinking fountain under the line of Chinese pistache trees. She's dressed like some kind of Indian princess rock star — jean shorts, fringy black vest, suede boots, and a few hunks of turquoise dangling from leather straps in her hair. Everyone always says how alike the two of us look, but it isn't totally true. Her eyes are so dark they look purple, while mine are plain and brown. Her hair, black as ink, is naturally sleek and shiny; mine is dark brown with some ugly natural high-lights, and it tangles very easily. The features we do have in common aren't beautiful. Our eyebrows are too full, our noses too sharp. While I try to smile at everyone I pass, my mother scowls. Everyone always says how beautiful she is, but looking at her now, I think she just looks tired and mean.

A lot of the boys are staring at her, and a couple of the dumb ones whistle. But she doesn't even react. Once her eyes have found me, they don't waver.

"Cheyenne," I say, walking straight up to her. Her eyes narrow, and I feel a small victory. The last time we were together, I still called her Mom.

She puts her hands to my cheeks. A current runs between us; it always has. "Look at you. I hardly recognize you without the weird makeup and black hair. You're beautiful, so grown up. Lacy, I'm so sorry about your dad." Lie number one.

"Are you?"

"Of course." Her eyes widen like I've hurt her, but I know it's an act. Nothing hurts her. I could pierce her flesh with jagged glass and she would only throw her head back in laughter. "I thought your father was a wonderful man." Lie number two.

What's it to you? I want to say. *You broke his heart again and again.* But I say nothing. I let her insincerity hover in the air between us.

"I can see that you're upset with me, Lacy. I'm sorry I had to leave you. But everything's different now. I want to prove it to you."

"If you want to prove anything, then let me stay in Chico," I say before I can stop myself. My eyes pool with tears of stupid desperation. "I want to stay here."

"Absolutely not." Her eyes flash. She's angry. I was too obvious. I wish I could take it back. "I'm your mother; you belong with me. Don't tell me you've gotten attached to that woman." She scoffs. "Listen, I know you like it here, but Sacramento is only an hour away. You'll be able to come back here to visit your friends, and that woman too if you like. You remember Sacramento, don't you?" She traces my jawbone with her fingernail. "You liked it. I have a new home there. It has a swimming pool and a little garden for you. I know you like planting things."

I don't wonder how she knows that — she's probably been watching us for days. But she doesn't know the half of it. She taught me those weird spells when I was little, but now I can harvest plants to cure nausea, to make sleep come, to pull pain and poison from the skin. But I can't stop time. I can't make her stop wanting me back.

"Please let me at least finish out this week of school." I practically beg.

"Negative. You're coming tonight."

CHAPTER THREE

The first time Cheyenne ever took me butterfly catching, we sprayed our hands with sugar water so they'd land right on our skin. It was spring then too. We were on the way back home from my dad's house in Chico, and we drove up to the very top of Table Mountain where the wildflowers were blooming. Everywhere you looked was color — the ground was yellow and purple and green; the sky was blue, and the air was filled with butterflies, big ones with orange-and-white wings. My mom handed me a yellow net — a small one made for a child. We ran through the fields, catching them in our nets and freeing them into glass mason jars. Afterward, we drank iced tea from a thermos as we drove back down the mountain to home. I held the jars in my lap, studying the slow flap of the butterflies' wings, the way they flitted against each other, and I longed to hold them again on the tips of my fingers. I thought maybe she'd let me set them free in the bedroom we shared. They would give us such beautiful dreams.

When we got home, she started melting beeswax in the double boiler. The kitchen smelled lovely, like springtime and candles. But then she opened a jar and lifted a butterfly out by its wing with tweezers, and she dipped it, still fluttering, into the melted wax. I screamed. I knew how it felt to be burned.

⁂

Anna sits on my bed, rubbing Mr. Murm's belly as he purrs, and staring at the ceiling while I pack dried herbs and essential oils into my patchwork overnight bag. The cloth handles are starting to fray, but it's too late for me to ask Anna to fix them. It doesn't matter anyway. It's not like I'm going to have any sleepovers at friends' houses anytime soon.

"I called your dad's lawyer," Anna says. "I have an appointment with her for Wednesday. I'm not sure there's anything I can do, but I will try."

"I know, Anna," I say. "Thank you."

"It's just not fair," she says, and for a moment she looks like a little girl about to throw a tantrum to get her way. *Please*, I silently beg, *be strong, be the adult.*

"Well. Everything happens for a reason, right?" I say, pulling the quote out of the air. It's something my dad always used to say. But is it true? If so, what was the reason for my dad dying? I shake my head. It can't be true. It's just that bad things happen. Bad mothers come back from the underworld, their sticky fingers snatching at their daughters. Little girls lose themselves, become bad. "Anna?" I sit beside her on my bed. Maybe Cheyenne is out there in the garden, maybe she's looking through the window right now, but I don't think so. I don't feel her out there. Besides, she had said she'd be at the school for at least another hour, talking to my teachers and getting my paperwork in order. "I'm scared."

"Oh, honey." Anna puts her arm around me, brushes my hair out of my eyes, and rests her chin on the top of my head. "If she hurts you, you call the police. And then you call me."

"No, that's not what I mean. It's that, when she's far away, I feel like I can be the person I want to be." Long ago, I decided Anna was a good role model for me, a person to hold up to the light. Anna who donates our garden's surplus of organic veggies to the food bank, who teaches free knitting workshops at the women's shelter. "As long as I'm with you, I can be good and do good things. But when I'm around her, I don't like the person I become. I don't want to be like her."

"Oh, Lacy. You aren't like her." She continues to hug me; she rocks me back and forth. But Anna must be forgetting how it was at first when I came to live with her and my dad. Like mother, like daughter. I have had to work hard at becoming someone good. I have had to reinvent myself. But I know that other me is still in there somewhere, just waiting for my mother to crack me open and set her free.

❖

By the time Cheyenne comes to pick me up, I feel like I might throw up. I should have known she'd be back for me one day, this woman who doesn't know how to be my mother. I remember the time she burned my wrist because I was asking too many questions. Another time she tied me to a tree so I couldn't wander away. I have so many memories of hurting at the hand of this woman who has a way of getting inside me, of making the pain rise to my skin so I just want to tear myself apart, so that sometimes I had to cut my skin open to let the pain out. But I haven't done that in a long time.

I have packed light: some sweaters and a blanket, my dried herbs packed in tissue, a sleep sachet, my dad's guitar, and the box containing my mermaid's eye and a feather from an egret who followed me home from school for three days straight. Also silver calligraphy ink Anna bought me at a store in Berkeley that displays fairy houses with intricate gardens and tree houses and gnomes and friendly mice. And I pack Mr. Murm, of course, in his little kitty carrier.

"Oh no," Cheyenne says the minute she sees the carrier. "No cats. No way."

"What? Mr. Murm is my best friend. He's all I have." I hate her. She takes everything away.

"Lacy, don't be dramatic. You have me, for God's sake. And it doesn't matter anyway. You're not bringing that cat."

"Please." My eyes pool again for about the millionth time and I bite my lip and I know I sound desperate. "Please, Mom."

She shakes her head. "I'm allergic. I'm sorry, but it's impossible."

I look to Anna, but what can she say? "I'll take care of him, honey. You can visit whenever you like."

She doesn't see the way my mother's eyes cut at her the moment she calls me honey. Note to Anna: Don't be counting on that visit.

⁜

Cheyenne's car looks so clean that it should probably still have that new car smell, except it seems saturated in Bad Apple perfume. It's like she sprayed it right into the upholstery. I don't even want to know what she did to land herself a new car. Seriously, I wouldn't be surprised to learn she stole it. Until yesterday, Cheyenne had been MIA for three years. After a year, my dad's attorney let us know she was in prison for extortion but a year later told us she'd been released, and we were all waiting for some sign that she was watching us again — burn marks on the lawn or wax butterflies on the doorstep. But nothing happened and I had started to relax. Stupid me.

We pass through the little towns on 99 peppered between the orchards and farmlands. Tiny towns with penny candy shops, fruit stands, and greasy-spoon diners. I wish we could stop at one of them the way Anna and my dad liked to do. Whenever we traveled, we would stop at the diners, try the milk shakes or the key lime pie. We would strike up conversations with the locals, learn where to go in town to find a snake charmer or a fairy garden or a great big ball of twine.

But those days are over.

Cheyenne's music is sad and gritty, old country songs I remember from long ago. She taps the wheel and sings along. Her voice is sweet and clear. There was a time when I loved listening to my mother sing. I'd forgotten how much I once loved it. I close my eyes and listen. But now I try to imagine it's Anna singing beside me instead.

It's almost working when my mother turns down the music and clears her throat. "You aren't a vegetarian, are you?" she asks. I open my eyes and see a lit-up burger joint ahead.

"No," I say. "I eat meat."

But Cheyenne keeps driving, right past the diner. "Good," she says. "I know that woman is a vegetarian. I don't want you trying to act like you're her. You're better than that."

"That woman has a name," I say. "Her name is Anna."

"Whatever." After a moment she says, "Just remember who your mother is. I am inside of you. I am your blood, your bones. You can't escape that."

What am I supposed to say to that? I say nothing. We drive in silence the rest of the way to Sacramento. I pull out individual strands of my hair and twist them around my fingers like dark rings.

✛

I'm expecting some dank and smelly apartment or hotel room in the ghetto like the ones we've lived in before. Instead, Cheyenne drives to a part of town I've never been to. She points to the right.

"That's Sac State," she says. "I might try to get in as a student in the fall."

"Really?" I say, and I almost laugh because the idea of her in school seems really bizarre. "And study what?"

"I don't know yet. It's just something I'm thinking about. Maybe psychology." While she shrugs, I think back to a psychologist I went to a few times when I first moved in with my dad and Anna. Her room was tidy and small, without degrees or books. Just an orange couch, a few nondescript paintings, and her desk. I liked her. When it was time for me to stop going, she told me I'd graduated and she gave me a diploma. I remember something she once said. "A lot of the crazies go into the field of psychology" was the gist of it.

Still, I guess it would probably be good for Cheyenne to take a few classes at the college. Not that she ever follows through on anything. She'll probably never enroll. In the dark, the college looks kind of spooky and empty; maybe that's what attracted her in the first place. The light changes and we turn into a neighborhood with a sign that says RIVER PARK. A few blocks in, I feel transported to someplace far from the Sacramento I've always known. In the past we've lived in some dodgy parts of town where there's graffiti everywhere and homeless people and kids on stolen bikes. Here, all the homes are lit with pretty porch lights and flags with sunflowers and storybook characters on them. Cheyenne pulls into the driveway of a big ranch-style house.

"Home sweet home," she says, cutting the engine.

"Really?" I can't help it. I'm skeptical. We've never lived anywhere this nice. "Do you share this place with other people?"

"What do you mean? No, it's all ours. Come inside."

"It's nice," I say, but I try to sound nonchalant. I don't want her to get the impression that I actually want to be here. Not that it matters.

Leaving all of my stuff in the trunk of the car, I follow Cheyenne up the steps. It's dark. Cheyenne begins flipping light switches on, but the house still seems dark. It's because of the walls. They're painted bloodred.

Dying plants droop in the corners. This woman can't even take care of a fern; how is she going to take care of me? Leaves the color of rotting bananas litter the hardwood floor. Poor plants. I'll be sure to water them in the morning and take them out into the sunshine.

There are wax butterflies in picture frames, lining the mantel, hanging from the ceiling by string. I shudder, choking back the memories, the smell of honey-burned wings. I think about what Cheyenne said to me in the car. *I am inside of you. You can't escape.* Even now I feel like it's somehow true, like her spirit is trying to force its way into my body.

"What's wrong with you?" Cheyenne asks, eyeing me.

"I'm not feeling so good. I feel like I might be sick." I feel the ghosts of dead butterflies fluttering in my stomach, flitting in and out of the shifting stones.

"There's your bathroom through there if you're going to yak," Cheyenne says, pointing to a closed door. Anna would hold me. She would rub my hair and back until I felt better.

"Okay." I push open the door and kneel at the toilet. I spit once, and then it all comes out, my school cafeteria pork burrito with crispitos and chocolate milk. I gag a few times and spit some more until my stomach stops heaving. Then I wipe my mouth and stand up. There's a toothbrush on the counter and I use it; my real one is still in the trunk of the car. *I'm okay*, I tell myself. It was only nerves.

When I was younger, I sometimes felt like she could control me. Even when she wasn't around. I would say things aloud, then wonder what they meant, where the words had come from. But I'm older now. She can't get inside my head. I won't let her.

Blinking, I survey the bathroom. It's sparse but clean. The walls are red, like the rest of the house. There's a new bar of glycerin soap on the sink. I splash water on my face, then go out, the taste of my vomit still thick and sour on my tongue.

"I put on some hot water for you. I remember you've always liked tea."

"Thank you." I say. "That's nice of you."

"Well, I'm your mother," Cheyenne says, and she does her best to smile, but her smile looks cold; it doesn't reach all the way up to her eyes. The eyes are the mirror to your soul, they say. If that's true, Cheyenne's soul is cold-blooded and dark.

It is true that I've always liked tea, so she's right about that. My friends think it's weird, but teenagers in England drink it; at least I think they do. Anyway, my dad says he used to give it to me when I was a baby because I had colic, so I guess I just grew up used to the taste of it. I find it comforting.

"I'll give you a tour," Cheyenne says. She doesn't wait for me to say yes or no. "This is the living room, obviously. Over there's the den." She points. "Your room. My room. My bathroom is in there too, but you won't need to go in there because you have your own bathroom." I've never had my own bathroom before, not even at my dad's and Anna's house. "This is the kitchen. Are you coming?"

Before following her, I look into my new bedroom. It is empty except for a mattress on the floor, a small dresser, and a pale orange butterfly with light blue spots hanging from the doorway. I'll be taking that down.

"Come on," Cheyenne says, and I follow her through the kitchen. "This is the backyard." She flicks on a porch light, illuminating a swimming pool, which is also lit from within. It is thick with mildew and debris. It looks more like a swamp than a pool, like an underwater shadow land where any number of murky creatures might lie in wait. Frogs croak beneath a line of rosebushes next to the fence. "And here's that place I was telling you about, where you can grow a garden. And I got you a bike; you'll need it to get to school. I'll drive you the first day, of course." I blink, surprised. She's never driven me to school before, first day or not. "Let me get you that tea."

Before following her back inside, I walk to the garden area. She had said a little spot, but it is larger than I'd imagined. I kneel next to it, a kidney-shaped bed with upturned soil. I take a fistful of soil and it's loamy and light. It's perfect.

Back in the kitchen, Cheyenne uncorks a bottle of her signature white wine with cherry blossoms on the bottle and takes a wineglass from a cupboard. "Here's tea." She hands me a mug with a few little balls or pods in a tea ball. "I'm going to change. I'll be right back."

The tea is good, an unfamiliar flavor. It makes me sleepy. Cheyenne comes out of her bedroom in a kimono, her glossy hair spilling around her shoulders, and yes, now I can see why people say she's beautiful. Maybe it's just harder for me to see because I know her so well. She pours wine into her glass.

"Cheers," she says, and she clinks my cup. "Should we go sit in the backyard? It's a nice night. We can talk, get to know each other again."

I study her, certain it's a tactic. She's never been this nice. Suddenly, my vision swims. The room seems to spin, and strange characters appear on the walls. Then they float from it, tall red demons with open mouths. I try to see them clearly, but when I focus, they drift like smoke to another part of the wall.

"Whoa," I say, blinking. "I guess I'm really tired."

"Are you okay?" She's hovering over me. Is she smiling? I can't focus on her face.

"I think I'd better go lie down," I say.

"Well, first I need you to do me a favor." Cheyenne takes her glass of wine to the screen door leading to the backyard. "Take out the kitchen trash. There's chicken in there, and it's going to start stinking."

"Okay," I say as she goes through the back door and out into the night.

"And lock the front door behind you," she hollers after me.

"Okay," I say, and hear my own voice echoing, *okay, okay, okay.* My eyes are beginning to shut. My body is so tired. I don't even know where she keeps the trash. Why doesn't she take it out? I'm not the one who ate chicken. But there is no arguing with my mother. I learned this long ago.

The trash is in the obvious spot, under the sink. I lift the yellow trash bag from the can. It's heavy, like there are dishes at the bottom. Very smart, Mom. Break a dish and throw it into a weak plastic bag. I hold the bag from the bottom and carry it to the front door.

Outside, the night is cool and the air feels fresh and clean. I find a Dumpster by the side of the driveway that says GARBAGE ONLY SOLAMENTE BASURA and try to lift the lid. It is heavy, I feel so weak, I am so tired. Yawning again, I lift the bag with my left hand and as I push on the Dumpster lid with my right, tiny shards of glass tear the bag. Suddenly glass pours out and cuts my chest. "Ow," I say, heaving the bag into the Dumpster. Blood stains my shirt and blooms outward like a black rose. I should care; this should feel like a very big deal, only I'm just so tired. Too tired to find my mom and tell her, or clean up in the bathroom, or even change into a fresh shirt. Instead, I stagger like a drunk from an old Western back into the house, into my room with the creepy walls. My stomach hurts too. I peel off my wet shirt and collapse onto the mattress, pulling the folded blanket at the foot up over me. All night long I dream of butterfly eyes, cans rolling down the street, and garbage swirling in the wind.

CHAPTER FOUR

Certain memories of my old life, when I was a kid and Cheyenne was my mother, blur and bleed into one another. I'm not sure what I dreamed and what was real. I have these images in my head. Memories, dreams — whatever they are, they seem real. Then again, I dreamed for many nights as a little kid that a witch sat beside my bed as I slept. In that dream, I would wake up and she would be looking at me, not saying anything. She scared me. I never found out what she wanted. That felt real, but it had to be a dream, so maybe these other things were dreams too.

The other things. I remember being in a field with my mom. There were cows in the field, and a tree. It was night, and she was digging a hole beneath the tree. Then she took thirteen black candles and placed them around the hole and started chanting.

She lit the candles and drew me near.

There was something in the hole she had dug. It looked slippery, and it moved, and it disgusted me. I turned away. She continued to chant, her voice rising in the night. She cut her hand with a knife, and her blood dripped to the dirt. The cows moved, strange dark objects. I was afraid of them too.

But I must have dreamed all that. If she were capable of sorcery and voodoo magic, Cheyenne would have done bad things to Anna. She would never have let my dad leave her in the first place.

❖

"I asked you to lock up." It is morning, and my mother is standing in the door frame of my new red bedroom. Sun streaks through the window, and the walls look less eerie than at night — the paint coverage is thin and I can see the white beneath the red.

"I thought I did." I struggle to remember. "I locked the front door. I took the trash out."

"I just went out to get the paper, and the front door was unlocked. The screen was wide open."

Cheyenne reads the paper? I rub my eyes.

"I'm really sorry," I say. "I thought I locked it."

" 'I thought' doesn't keep the bad guys out. Get up," Cheyenne says. "We need to get you some new clothes for school."

I look down at my crumpled shirt on the floor beside my bed.

"Wait," I say, and Cheyenne pauses. I want to tell her about how the glass cut me last night. But when I pull the blanket away from me like a tent and look down, everything looks normal. I pick up my shirt from the floor. There are no bloodstains, and no glass falls to the ground. Did I dream it? "Never mind," I say. "I mean I thought . . . but never mind."

Cheyenne looks at me for a minute. "You okay?" she finally asks.

"I think so." She looks at me with one eyebrow raised, that look she always gives me that makes me feel like I'm crazy. "Sorry," I say, although I don't really know what it is I'm apologizing for.

"Well," she finally says. "Let's get going before the shops fill."

35

⁙

I remember a party my mother once threw. It was late at night and mostly men, but there were women in gowns there too. Almost all of them at the party wore masks. Plume feathers and plastic dog and rabbit heads covering their faces. There was a devil with a shiny red face and a goatee — I kept my distance from him.

The music was loud in our little apartment and I waited for the police to come and make everyone go home, but they never did, not on that night. There was a fishbowl of pills that looked like candy on the table. I wanted some of the candy, but a man in one of those feathered masks took me by the arm and explained that it would make me sick. The pills would make me hallucinate, he said, which meant I'd see things that weren't there, like maybe monsters and giant snakes with big teeth.

But I had watched my mother take a handful.

After that I stayed right beside her, because I wanted to be there if she needed me. I would tell her the snakes and monsters weren't real. I'd rub her head and make her a chain of paper dolls — a tiny one she could wear as a necklace or as a crown around her head.

I waited for the police to come. At other parties, on other nights, they would be here by now.

My mother was wearing a long green dress like a mermaid, and her mask was gold with black beading and rhinestones. She lay back against the green couch we'd found on the sidewalk the week before, and she sang along to the music that was blaring up from the stereo. Her voice was so pretty, like a cartoon princess almost. She was sweating and I was rubbing her arm. But then a man in a top hat came and lifted me off the couch.

"Go to bed, little girl," he said. He had an accent, maybe French or Italian. "This is no kind of place for a child."

I stood there, but he reached down and gently lifted my mother in his arms, and when he bent over, he hit me with his butt and I staggered backward into the coffee table, spilling all the drinks. Then people were yelling at me and the man was carrying my mother into her bedroom and closing the door, and when I tried it, it was locked.

I went to the fishbowl and took a piece of the candy, but it tasted awful and I spit it out.

"No kind of place for a child," the man had said. I've remembered that forever after.

❖

The interior of Cheyenne's car no longer smells like her perfume. There is a clean smell now, like lemons and leather. Cheyenne herself is only lightly scented, and she's dressed in a pale pink cardigan and white blouse. Her hair is pulled back in a neat ponytail. She looks like someone else's mother.

"Cheyenne," I say, and she tightens her grip on the steering wheel. "You don't have to buy me new clothes. I have clothes."

"Don't be silly. This is one of the pleasures of being a mother." This is one of the pleasures of being controlling. "It's been too long since we've gone shopping together. Besides, I've seen the stuff you wear. That might work in Chico, but Sacramento is a big city. It's the capital of California you know. People here don't dress like they're going out to pick berries or take a ride on a hay wagon." I look down at the jeans and gray sweater I changed into this morning. Do I really look that bad, like a country bumpkin, like a hick?

"I like the way I dress." I make one last attempt, but I hear how I sound, and I shut my mouth. She is going to win this one.

"Anyway, I've never heard of a teenage girl who doesn't like shopping for new clothes," she says.

She pulls into a parking lot with an Oil and Lube, a tire place, and a nail salon. "Does the car need its nails done?" I ask.

"Ha-ha. There's a little shop in back. It's very cool. And I happen to be friends with the owner."

I follow Cheyenne past the tire store to a little black cottage with a red picket fence. The garden inside the fence is lush with spinach and chard, hanging nasturtiums, and spider plants. We go through the gate and up the stone path, past gargoyles with fierce red eyes and a fountain of a stone woman whose many breasts spit water.

I raise my eyebrows, but Cheyenne doesn't seem to notice that this place is creep-o-rama. She opens the glass-and-iron door and walks right in. The sign above the shop reads DEMETER'S DAUGHTER.

"Myrna?" Cheyenne calls out after I've stepped inside. Inside is even creepier than out. Little mice that look real are posed in glass cases, each depicting a different scene. The first scene is childbirth. A mouse with her legs caught in stirrups is bleeding while a doctor mouse whose face is virtually hidden by a mask holds a scalpel. In another case, a murder is taking place. A mouse with a top hat and cloak stabs at a scantily clad female mouse on a cobblestone street. Her blood runs in rivulets and sinks into the cracks. At first it makes me think of the magical store in Berkeley where Anna bought me my silver calligraphy ink, but this is different, the dark side of a similar coin.

Real-looking crows hover over mirrors and paintings of dark goddesses with burned wings. A woman, Myrna I guess, comes through a beaded curtain in the back.

"Cheyenne." She smiles tightly, but when she sees me, her face relaxes and her smile widens. "Hi, Lacy. Do you remember me? Probably not, it's been so long. I used to babysit you. Your mom and I are old friends."

She does look familiar to me although I can't place her in any memory. She's thin and pretty with wispy bleach-blond hair, red lips, and blue jeans. "Nice to meet you," I say. "Again."

"I saw you admiring the crows. Do you like them? My husband is into taxidermy. They're all real. You can hold one if you like."

"Oh no, thank you." If I were the girl I used to be, I might say yes, but the truth is, the big black dead birds creep me out almost as much as the butterflies encased in wax.

"Actually, Lacy loves science." Cheyenne turns to me. "This kind of thing should be right up your alley."

"Well, I love botany," I say, more to Myrna than Cheyenne. "You know, the study of plants. But my friends and I walked out when it was time to dissect frogs in seventh grade."

"Really? Good for you. I would never have had the nerve to do that when I was young." Myrna smiles and I smile too, not mentioning the fact that my teacher, in the days leading up to the dissection, told us about his own seventh-grade biology walkout, and most of us took that as a green light to follow suit.

"The thing is," Myrna adds, and I have the feeling she's trying to align herself with me, "these guys die naturally. We don't believe in harming live objects. These are roadkill." She smiles brightly.

"Oh."

"And then the mice are mostly from friends, you know, they catch them in traps in their homes. We don't endorse that, but we're happy to take them off their hands."

I nod, trying not to look grossed out. Roadkill and glue traps. Can we change the subject, please?

"Myrna, Lacy is starting school here on Monday, and she doesn't want her first impression to be that she's a pumpkin farmer from wherever it is pumpkins are farmed."

"Um, they're farmed right here in California," I say.

"Well, excuse me for not knowing."

"Like haven't you ever seen a pumpkin patch?" I ask. Cheyenne puts her hand on the back of my neck and pinches. "Ow!" I turn to glare at her. Myrna watches us, then turns away. There's something strange about this woman, and that's aside from the shop of dead things. It's like it's important to her that we're really comfortable and happy in this weird little shop, and the way she ignores us now feels like an admonishment. I feel as though I've fallen down the rabbit hole.

"Yes," Myrna finally says. "First impressions are important. Come with me." I follow her past racks of curiosities, like glitter skull sugar bowls and daguerreotypes — old cracking yellow photos of unsmiling girls.

In the clothing section of the store, she shows me black skirts and black tops and black scarves and black hats. Wearing this stuff would be like dressing for a funeral every day. Since my dad died, I haven't been wearing much black. I don't see the point of mourning clothes. When you lose someone, your mood and your spirit are already black. Why drape your body in all that too?

40

But all the clothes in the shop are some shade of black, and I can't help but find myself enchanted. The clothing is beautiful, hand-stitched with gossamer threads. The fabrics are soft and thick, like new skin. "Do you make these?" I ask Myrna.

"My labor of love. Yes, they're all originals. Do you like them?"

"They're beautiful." I am actually a little breathless. "But, Cheyenne, we can't afford these." I show her a three-hundred-dollar price tag.

"No, no," Myrna says, and something razor sharp flashes in her eyes. "Your mom and I go way back. And I am indebted to her. Please" — she takes a pile of clothes from the rack — "try these on."

In the dressing room I study myself in the mirror. I've lost a lot of weight since my dad died. I've always been small, and Shell and Mechelle used to make fun of me freshman year because I ate frozen cheesecakes dipped in chocolate on a stick every day for lunch, and I never gained a pound. But now I look sick, breakable. My scars from old cuttings on my legs are raised and white, and I try not to look at them because they remind me of how sad and awful and desperate I used to feel. I look like shit.

Putting the first dress on, I expect to look like a little kid playing dress-up or some paper doll in the wrong dress, but I don't. I look strong. I look like a girl who can see the magic in the everyday, who can even use it to make things better sometimes. I twirl. I look good.

By the time we leave, I have a mountain of beautiful new clothing. Plumed cocktail dresses I will never wear. Fairy gloves stitched with tiny silken rosettes. Glittery scarves and thick soft tights. It seems wasteful, but at the same time, it is intoxicating.

Best of all is a jeweled black rose necklace on a gold chain. I wanted it the second I saw it, and I couldn't believe when Cheyenne said yes. "You have sophisticated tastes," she told me, nodding appreciatively, and for a moment, I felt almost proud. The necklace hangs halfway down my chest, so the rose falls just at my heart.

It is the loveliest thing I've ever had.

⁘

After shopping, my mother takes me out to lunch. We go to a French café, order pâté and iced tea and salad and brie. I have never spent time with my mother this way. She has never taken me shopping for clothes; she has never taken me anywhere for lunch except McDonald's. Maybe she really has changed. Maybe she really is trying.

"Thank you for the clothes, and the necklace." I run the rose along the gold chain. "Did you know gold and copper are the only metals that aren't silver in color?" Random chemistry fact. Cheyenne gives me a look that you'd give to indulge a child who is telling a lie.

"You're welcome," she says.

"So what's the likelihood of you letting me stay home from school tomorrow?" I ask.

"I don't care if you go to school," she says, "but I think the state does. We're playing by the rules this time, kiddo."

"I could homeschool. That's allowed."

"I work all night and I sleep during the day. I don't need some moody teenager playing loud music and slamming her door all day long."

"I don't . . . That isn't me."

"How would I know? I haven't seen you in three years."

I start to remind her of the reason for this, then reconsider. The reason, of course, is that when I was thirteen, she disappeared. Just stopped coming home. So that finally, after three days, I called my dad, who took me to live with him and Anna.

"Where did you go, when you disappeared?" I ask instead. But she gives me a sharp look and leans forward.

"The past is the past," she says coldly. "Can we move on?"

"Sorry," I say, and the word tumbles slippery and toxic as gasoline. She pulls a small mirror from her purse and examines her lips.

"Good," she says, and snaps the mirror shut.

CHAPTER FIVE

When my mother disappeared, I lived off salami, beans, and ketchup for three days. I didn't have money for cafeteria lunch, so I stole chips and chocolate milk from the aluminum racks at school. I did not allow myself to believe that she wouldn't be back for me. We were going to Paris together. She wouldn't leave me behind.

But the nights were scary. Even though I was a tough girl, with jet-black hair and smoky eyes, my imagination was still wicked and wild. We hadn't had electricity for weeks, so I had to burn candles if I wanted to see after dark. I envisioned mass murderers and poltergeists. I slept in my mom's bed, beneath all her blankets. I slept with my old stuffed teddy bear. All night I waited, beneath the covers, waiting for the sound of her, at the driveway, at the door, by my side.

❖

My father once took me on a midnight canoe trip down the American River. The moon hung low and orange in the sky. We paddled over to an island, and he lit a fire with flint and steel. In the distance, I saw something out of the corner of my eye, a thing of light and movement. He saw it too, and we followed it, but soon it had disappeared, leaving us to wonder if we had imagined it all.

He boiled a pot of hot water over the fire and we drank powdered hot chocolate from metal cups, and I fell asleep with my head in his lap. When I woke up, there were tiny slips of paper scattered around the small island. While my dad slept, I moved from paper to paper, picking each one up and reading it. *"If you're ever lonely,"* the little notes said, *"and looking for friends" "Look beneath egg nests and shells" "We wear camouflage hats" "To hide from big folk" "But you, we consider our pal."*

I kept the notes in a ceramic fish on my dresser for years. But of course, by the time my mom disappeared, I no longer believed in fairies or enchantment. The notes, I knew, were faked by a loving father, and I threw them away one day when I was cleaning out my room.

⁘

Later, several hours after lunch at the French café, I kneel beside my garden in the backyard and dig into the soil with my hands. Surrounding me are my new little herbs in plastic cartons — lavender, rosemary, mint, sage, and thyme. Protection, love, prosperity, comfort, and happiness. I whisper good intentions to them as I tap at the sides of their containers to loosen their soil. The screen door slides open and Cheyenne comes out, wearing a black cropped bustier top and Mardi Gras beads. "Here's money for pizza," she says, holding out a crumpled twenty. "Make me a list of what you eat, and I'll go shopping for you. You're going to be on your own most nights for dinner."

"Why? Where are you going to be?"

"Work. Ever heard of it? Pays the bills?"

"Sorry, I . . . wasn't thinking. What type of job do you have?"

"Bartender. Lousy pay, decent tips. Lots of men." She runs her tongue across her teeth, joking, I hope. "I have to go, okay?"

"Okay," I say, a little relieved. At least she has a job. Maybe we really are going to be okay.

After she leaves, I turn back to my garden and put the little plants in the ground. They look sweet and hopeful — the lavender waving its purple stalks in the breeze. The frogs begin their late-afternoon croaking from the rosebushes. After a while, I go back inside, turn on all the lights, and call the pizza place. For a moment, I consider ordering something good and vegetarian, like Anna would. But when I open my mouth, it asks for a large pepperoni with sausage.

❖

I pop the screen from my window and hide it at the side of the house. I don't like screens in windows. I like full access to the night. As the spring sun sets, turning the sky to a tie-dye of purple night and yellow clouds tinged with orange, I light a candle and eat the pizza at my window, listening to frogsong.

My phone chirps (the ringtone set to CRICKETS) and I pick up. Anna.

"Hey," I say, my mouth still full.

"Hi, Lacy. I hope I'm not disturbing you. Is Cheyenne there?"

"No, she's at work." I wipe my mouth with a napkin.

"Work? She actually has a job?"

"Yeah. She has a car, and a real house. She took me shopping."

"I wonder who she's stealing money from this time."

"I don't know." Even though I had the same thought, I don't like hearing it from Anna. Cheyenne is still my mother, and there are some things other people aren't allowed to say. Mothers are off-limits. I feel a surge of protection toward her, and I have to remind myself how much I love Anna too.

"How are you?" I ask.

"Well, it's lonely around here, but Mr. Murm is keeping me company."

"Good," I say, but it makes me sad. Anna and Mr. Murm. I miss them both. The candle flickers at my window. I look outside at the night, now a pure velvety purple. Stars and planets are beginning to appear like pinpricks in fabric held up to the light. I miss everyone.

⁜

My father had a sense of humor that not everyone understood. Sometimes, around friends, he'd make some joke and everyone would stare at him, not daring to laugh, not sure whether or not he was joking. But I always knew. I'd lean against him, cracking up. "You're the only one who gets me," he'd often say.

He was like a wolf. A little bit wild. A little untamed. But he was playful, and silly, and I loved him. I loved him so much.

He played guitar and sometimes he dressed in a chicken suit. The night is now totally dark. I lie in bed, tears pooling on my pillow. When I wake up, my eyes will be so puffy and pink, I know.

⁜

Cheyenne driving first thing in the morning is not an event I have ever in my lifetime enjoyed. She looks like she's about to fall asleep at the wheel, and her hands are shaking, and she's almost rear-ended three cars. When we get to my new high school, she pulls up behind a city bus and rests her head on the steering wheel. I wait, unsure what to do.

"Are you dropping me off here?" I ask.

"Yes," she says, her head still down.

"Okay. Well. Um. Get some rest."

"Mmmph."

I get out of the car and start walking through the parking lot. I stumble over an upturned chunk of asphalt and try to recover, hoping no one saw. I feel so conspicuous in my new clothes — an eyelet summer dress, polka-dot knee socks, and Eskimo boots (all in shades of black, of course). No one is dressed like me. Everyone in the parking lot is wearing jeans or shorts. They dress just like everyone does in Chico.

It's been so long since I've been completely uprooted, since I've had to start a new school where I know nobody. I wish I could just vanish. Better yet, I wish I were the old Lacy, with my smoky eyes and stolen bomber jacket. Instead, I am New Girl in a five-hundred-dollar dress. I think I'm the only white person at this school. But no, there are others. I am not alone in my whiteness. I am only alone in my aloneness.

At the office, I am given my class schedule and locker assignment. First period, English. I don't want to look like a total loser by being the first one there. Then again, I don't want to wander the halls alone. I head to Room C10.

Surprisingly, I'm not the only one there. A group of kids sit near the middle of the room, inspecting a tattoo on one of the girls' forearms. The girl has gorgeous auburn hair piled on top of her head like a fountain. She has dark skin and a sprinkling of freckles across her face.

"It's a Taino symbol for *sun*," the girl is saying. "I wanted it bigger, but my arms are too small."

"It's cute," says one of her friends, and the tattoo girl squinches up her face and looks at her disdainfully.

"It's not cute, it's tribal. Ancient people would say this tattoo puts me closer to the gods."

"Oh no, avert your eyes, gods," says a boy with dark curly hair and eyes that remind me of a cat. They are a strange greenish-yellow — more green than yellow, but still there is something feline-esque about them. "Olive's coming closer and she isn't wearing underwear."

"Shut up!" The girl with the tattoo, Olive, punches him in the arm, but I can tell she's a little flattered that he's thinking about her underwear or lack thereof. I wonder if they're dating or if they're just that kind of friends. I think of Zach and feel a pang. Sometimes it really did feel like we were on our way to becoming more than friends. Now I'll never get to find out.

The classroom begins to fill up, even though the bell hasn't rung yet. Olive looks at me, and the others follow her gaze, but she looks away and they do too. She continues to show her tattoo to anyone who will look, and everyone wants to look, even though, as far as I can tell, it's just a black circle with a simple face inside. I hover at the back of the classroom. Hopefully, when the teacher comes (Mrs. Kesey, according to my schedule), she will see me and find a place for me to sit.

The bell rings and more students shuffle in followed by a white pregnant woman with red blotchy skin and stringy blond hair. She looks like the kind of teacher who would go home crying after the first day, yet the way she walks, the way she sits on her desk at the front of the room, exudes a quiet confidence.

"Okay, everyone," she says. Her eyes find me at the back of the room and she smiles. "All kinds of news today. Olive got a new tattoo." Olive waves like a princess, her wrist straight but her hand rotating side to side. "Very nice. And we have a new student. Hi there," she says to me, and she smiles widely. "You must be Lacy." I nod. "Welcome. Lacy comes to us from Chico, just about . . . ninety miles north?" I nod again.

"Chico State's a party school," someone says in a fake grown-up man voice from the front of the room.

"Chico State's awesome." The boy with the curly hair fixes his cat eyes on me. "Pioneer Days, right? Party." He throws a half-assed fist bump in my direction, and I blink at him. I have no idea what he's talking about. Olive looks at me with what appears to be disdain, although I can't imagine why. I haven't said a word yet.

"Pioneer Days were shut down in the eighties, Mr. MacLachan, due to *excessive* partying," the teacher says.

"Excessive partying," the boy repeats admiringly, and he and his friends snicker. The teacher carries on as though she doesn't hear him.

"Okay, Lacy, so you can sit" — she looks behind herself at something on her desk — "right there next to Mr. Davis. Mr. Davis, raise your hand." A boy in a football jersey raises his hand and his eyebrows, smiling politely or condescendingly, I can't tell which. I walk forward and take the seat.

A chubby boy with glasses who sits in the front row waves at me. He has orange socks around his hands, cut like fingerless gloves. Olive continues to look at me coolly. I stare back at her. Then I wave at the kid in front. He grins broadly. Maybe he's special ed or something.

❖

50

After class, Olive and her crew walk out of the room together like an amorphous mass. But first the boy with the yellow eyes glances at me, and he nods, closing his eyes and smiling slightly.

The chubby boy from the front of the room comes over. "Lacy, oh my gosh, how are you?"

"Do I know you?"

"Lacy Fin, right? I'm Martin Molinero. We used to be neighbors."

"Oh my God!" I look at Martin, trying to see in him the little boy I used to know. Martin and I lived in the same apartment complex when we were nine. But he was skinny then, a little scrap of a boy who was terrified of his father. One time, after Martin forgot to bring his raincoat to school, his dad made him stand in his underwear in the rain until the sun went down. He had to stand in the apartment complex parking lot where we could all see him. That day he wouldn't talk to me, or even look at me. It was my loneliest day. Other days, we spent hours together, trading bottle caps or listening to the big kids who called each other the N-word at the park near where we lived.

"Wow, Lacy. You look exactly like your mom. I used to have such a big crush on her."

"You did?" My hand goes self-consciously to my hair.

"Don't worry," Martin says quickly. "I'm not so much into girls anymore, if you know what I mean."

"Oh," I say, and, as if from another part of my brain, an ugly word forms. A horrible word that sounds like hate and makes me cringe even though I didn't say it out loud.

Where did that come from? I bite my tongue hard so that I can taste blood, and my eyes well with tears. It's happening.

I used to be mean. I was one of those girls. The kind who loved to deliver bad news. I was the girl who would flirt with your boyfriend, and if you were my best friend, even better. I would steal from other kids' desks, and I would lie about it to their faces. I was an angry old witch in a thirteen-year-old's body. But I've changed. I'm not like that anymore. I am a good friend. I am a good person.

✜

At lunch, I meet Martin in the cafeteria, over by the line for Taco Queen. Olive and her friends are standing nearby too, the girls sipping from Diet Cokes and the boys singing an off-tune rendition of the Beatles' "Rocky Raccoon."

"How's your first day so far?" Martin asks me.

"It's okay." I tilt my head, thinking about what more I can say. "I miss my friends." And this school smells funny, like fish. My old school smelled fine. And my locker has pink and green gum stuck to the back wall. And I'm having mean thoughts again, and I don't know how long it will be before I start acting like a total bitch and hating everything and cutting myself and being completely out of control.

"That sucks. I'm sure it was hard to leave your friends," Martin says, sighing in sympathy, and I struggle to get ahold of myself. "Well, are you buying food? We can go sit outside. I'm on a white foods diet. Milk and vanilla yogurt, I guess." He looks at the cartons skeptically before reaching for them.

"A white foods diet? I've never heard of it."

"I made it up. Last week it was Christmas foods. I like to mix it up."

I smile. We move into the line and I start reading the menu overhead.

"You could get a queso blanco quesadilla," I suggest.

"Nice," Martin says, putting back the cup of yogurt. "I might have starved."

"Oh, look," someone says, and I feel Martin tense beside me. It's Olive. "Martin has a little friend. Hey, new girl. You might want to rethink your social standing. Reputations are made very quickly around here."

"Then I'll make sure if I get a tattoo, it won't look like it was done by a first grader," I say, my voice like venom. I don't know when it happened, but the shell has cracked. The bad me is being reborn.

❖

"Let me see your schedule," Martin says. We are eating our lunches out in "the plaza," which is really just a strip of grass with some trees. I pull the wrinkled schedule from my notebook and hand it to him.

"Oh, look, seventh-period chem with Mrs. Burke. I'm in that class!" He claps his hands together. "You can be my lab partner!"

"I can? You don't already have one?"

"Nope." Come to think of it, it does not appear that Martin has any friends at all. I don't know how it's possible to be into the spring of junior year and not have a single friend, but this seems to be the case with Martin.

Which doesn't make any sense. He's funny and smart. He's comfortable to be around. You would think a guy like that would know lots of people.

"It's because of Olive," Martin says, evidently reading my thoughts. "She's the reason no one will talk to me."

"How come?"

"She hates me because I beat her in the sixth-grade spelling bee. She warned me beforehand that if I didn't let her win, she'd make my life miserable. I didn't believe her. But don't worry; I'm not miserable. The people at this school are mindless zombies. Only stupid people would put Olive and her friends on a pedestal."

"Agreed," I say, watching the zombies circle around their queen, while Olive holds court with an apple in her hand. The boy with the yellow eyes catches my eye. He winks at me before I have a chance to look away.

⁘

After lunch is gym glass. Why on earth would anyone schedule PE after lunch? Gym is humiliating enough without upchucking your chimichanga all over the floor.

Before class, I am given a uniform to wear: shorts and a T-shirt with a bubble in which I am supposed to write my name with permanent ink. The uniform is too big for me, but all they had left were larges. I roll the waist of the shorts over itself so they won't fall off while I'm doing whatever it is they do in gym class in Sacramento.

What they do, as it turns out, is volleyball. Great. I am terrible at every sport that involves a ball, but volleyball is probably my least favorite. The way those balls fly straight at your head. The way every girl on your team groans when you miss. And I always miss.

On the bright side, I am new here. No one knows that I suck at sports. And I have reinvented myself before. Maybe today will be the day I master volleyball.

Just as Mrs. Anderson has us line up so we can pick teams, Olive comes sailing into the gymnasium. The girls in line seem to perk up. The arms of her T-shirt are rolled up, presumably so we can all admire her new tattoo.

"Miss Santiago," says the teacher. "You're late."

"Sorry," Olive says like she isn't sorry at all.

"Okay, we're about to pick teams." Mrs. Anderson assigns captains, and, surprise of surprises, I am picked last.

A girl on my team serves the ball. It flies over the net, and the other team assumes it will be out-of-bounds, but it lands just inside the line. Our team cheers. Our server serves again. This time they're ready for it. Pass, set, hit, it crosses the net and comes, of course, straight to me. I cover my face with my hands. The ball hits my hands, and my team is yelling at me. I am mortified, but I try to shake it off.

Now the other team serves. It goes to one of Olive's friends, who passes it to Olive. But instead of setting it, Olive hits, hard, aiming for my head. And makes perfect contact.

It is official. I am the newest loser at school.

✤

Last period of the day is chemistry, my always and forever favorite class. I love chem, I love botany, I love everything science. I loved biology. I intend to love physics. I love the language of science, chock-full of terrific-sounding words like *Bunsen burner* and *electron* and *harmonic motion*. The fact that matter and light can be both wave and particle. If I'm ever in a band, I'm going to call it Wave Particle Duality.

By the time I get to class, Martin is already sitting at his desk, and I smile and take the seat beside him.

"Hey, lab buddy," he says. The class files in, and I get the best news of the day: Olive isn't in it, and neither are any of her friends.

The teacher, Mrs. Burke, closes the door behind her. The rest of the hour is a lovely blur of metals and alloys, molecular theory and periodic law and chemical bonding.

⁘

After school, Cheyenne is not waiting for me by the bus stop, and it occurs to me that we never discussed how I'd get home. The bike, she'd told me, was for getting to and from school, but since she drove me this morning, I am bikeless. Also, there is the small fact that I don't know how to get back to River Park.

You would think I could just walk in the direction of the river, which might seem like a simple thing in most cities, but is not a viable option in Sacramento. For one thing, there are two rivers that run through town, and the streets wind and curve so that you're always changing direction.

I start walking until I see a sign that says csus. This is Sac State, and I know we don't live too far from there. I walk until I find the campus, and then I sit beneath the ginkgo trees. I think of Chico, of the mermaid's eye I found with Anna, of the goat boy on the river. Of the magic that was there, until my dad died.

Here, there is no magic. Only another girl lost in a strange part of a new town. A girl who used to be bad. That old story.

CHAPTER SIX

Our last name is Fin, like the fin on a fish, like a mermaid, scales and salt. The name belongs to all of us, Cheyenne, my dad, and me. Anna took it when she married him, so we are all of us Fins. The fins are what keep a fish stable, what keep it from rolling out of control. And yet, we Fins, we are always rolling, like kids down a hill, faster and faster as we fly toward the bottom.

I don't remember a time without Anna, although there was one. She didn't meet my dad until I was four, but I don't have much memory of that time. From the time I was two and my parents divorced, I bounced back and forth between my mom's house and my dad's. It wasn't until I started kindergarten that Cheyenne asked the court for, and received, full custody.

I remember my dad and Anna's wedding. They were married in the spring the year I was seven. The wildflowers were blooming and the creek was high. The teepee we sometimes stayed in was covered in fairy lights, and Tibetan prayer flags hung from the trees. Anna made me my dress and a crown of poppies and lupine. Our friends the Treehuggers were playing their music, and apple blossoms fell from above.

Before the wedding, my mom had told me she was scared Anna was trying to replace her. She made me swear that I would never call her Mom. As though I ever would. As though Anna would ever have wanted me to. Cheyenne was afraid they would try to take me away. "Your dad thinks I'm unfit," she would tell me. I would sit beside her and pat her hair. She was afraid I would forget her. I swore I would never ever forget her, not if terrorists tortured me with bamboo under my fingernails. Not if stars ripped across the black sky and crashed onto the earth in a fiery explosion of gas.

⁌

I am about to give up, just cut my losses and become a homeless wanderer through the streets of Sacramento, when I see a tire shop that looks familiar. When I see the crimson of the red picket fence, I duck my head and whisper yes in relief. My backpack is getting heavy and I'm starved.

I sludge through the gate, past the weird fountains, and up to the door to Myrna's shop. Myrna is behind the counter. When she sees me, she grins.

"Lacy," she says. "I had a feeling I'd see you again soon. I made cookies and I can put on some tea. What kind do you like? Are you hungry?"

"Sure," I say. "Whatever kind of tea you have." She smiles again and hurries me through the beaded curtain and into a little kitchen area in the back. "This used to be a house," she tells me. "Can't you imagine living here? It's so cozy."

I try to imagine how the kitchen would look without the black walls and spiderweb curtains, marble floors and glittering skulls. I suppose, if slicked with some yellow paint, it could be considered cozy. I sit at the table — a sheet of glass perched on a weird metal monster — and Myrna pours me a cup of tea.

"I like your table," I say.

"Isn't it awesome? It's an alien table. My husband got it for me for my birthday."

"You have . . . different tastes."

"I'm drawn to the macabre. The funny thing is, our house doesn't look anything like this. I'd be afraid to sleep around all these monsters and ghouls."

"Really?"

"Oh yeah. I think it's that fear that made me want a shop like this." She brings a plate of cookies to the table and sits down. "You know, we always want to dance face-to-face with our demons, but maybe not late at night. What brings you today?"

"I was lost," I admit.

"I can give you a ride home. If you don't feel like walking."

"That's okay. You have your store to watch."

"Hmm. Yeah, well. You might have noticed I don't get a lot of clientele."

"Why not? Your stuff's amazing." I finger the rose necklace that falls at my heart. "Even if people weren't here to shop, you'd think they'd come to look around."

"It used to be like that. Maybe they can sense that my heart's not really in it anymore." Myrna laughs to herself, a bitter secret laugh that I know not to question. She folds her arms around herself and crosses her legs. She's wearing one of her fabulous black sweaters, black jeans, and boots, but she looks cold, and sad. I sip at my tea, which is hot and surprisingly normal: peppermint. I expected roadkill oolong or something.

"My stepmother, Anna, would like it here. Not that she's into the macabre; she's not. But she loves things that are handmade."

"Oh?" I should probably stop talking. I know Myrna and my mom are friends, and I don't want Myrna telling her I came to her shop and told her all about Anna. But I also want Myrna to know. I feel like she should know where my loyalties are.

"She sells her stuff too, but not in a shop like this. She sells online, and then a bunch of shops around the country sell her stuff. She makes paper crafts, mostly. But she also knits, and she sews, but not by hand like you. She uses a sewing machine."

"Do you miss her?" Myrna asks, and I feel that the question is genuine. But I know you can't trust anyone. I know this is my cue to go.

"Nah," I say. "I have my mom now. She's great too. I have to get going. Can you tell me how to get home?" Myrna walks me back through the shop and points me in the right direction.

"If you hit the river," she says, "you've gone too far."

"Thanks," I say. "And thanks for the tea." Myrna looks so sad. I almost want to go back and give her a hug. But instead, I hurry through the red picket fence and backtrack around the corner toward the river.

❖

At first, of course, I turned on Anna, just as my mom wanted me to. I wore her dress and danced at the wedding, mostly because I didn't want my dad and the Treehuggers to see me act out. But I would tell her I hated her whenever we were alone. I stole lipstick from her dresser and mashed it up to make fake potions that I fed to my dolls. I put sugar syrup in her perfume so she'd be followed by bees and wasps. I gave her a sleep sachet of dark herbs for her birthday. She took it so sweetly, and afterward I felt bad. I stole it back, afraid it would hurt her. I didn't like her, but I didn't want to seriously hurt her.

My dad tried to talk to me, but he couldn't reach me. I refused to change my mind. I was loyal to my mother, and I wouldn't back down. The ideas were my own, and I felt proud because I knew my mother would be too. Anna never said a word about any of it. She tried to be nice, even though I was so awful. She told me once that she had lost the sleep sachet I made her. She apologized for her carelessness and asked if I might make her another. I considered making a real one, with rose petals and lavender, but in the end I never did.

After they were married, we would always go to visit the Treehuggers on pagan holidays, like solstice and Brigit and Lammas. The Treehuggers are my dad's friends from college — Jim, Miguel, and Grampy, who is the same age as the others. They're all into backpacking and urban farming, and they try to live off the land as well as they can. They have their own property, where we used to live, and they have the teepee and they love making things like earth ovens and outdoor cob fireplaces. They just care about having fun and making music. And me. They care about me.

They would take me hiking sometimes up Monkey Face in Upper Bidwell Park. Miguel has a huge dog named Bear, and with his big paws, he'd sound like a horse running up the trail. We would all eat homemade granola bars or trail mix and drink iced tea from a thermos, and they'd make up songs about me or we'd all fall asleep in the sun on top of the rock beside the face, which is just as high as the face but easier to fit on. They always wanted me to see the monkey in the rock, but I never really did. To me it just looked like rocks. From up there, Horseshoe Lake really is shaped like a horseshoe, and orange and green moss grows on the rocks and there are black birds with red chests and white wings. There is magic up there too.

Once, during a meteor shower, they took me for a night hike. We climbed so close to the stars, it felt like maybe we'd uncrack all the secrets of the universe. Like maybe they really would come raining down on us and we could catch the secrets in our bare hands. Another time, while the Treehuggers were down at the creek, a tiny woman in an old-fashioned dress walked past me, carrying a basket of St. John's wort. When I asked her what she was going to use it for, she smiled at me but didn't answer. Then she disappeared down the trail. I sometimes wonder if she was the ghost of Annie Bidwell, the woman who gave the park to the city of Chico when she died. Like me, she was a botanist, and she worried about the future of the local Mechoopda Indians.

The Treehuggers took me to Melody Records and Ital Imports and taught me which used tapes and records to buy. Dylan and Joplin and Radiohead. The Treehuggers were like my uncles. They didn't care if I was a mean little girl or an ugly hard teen who stole bomber jackets. Maybe they just didn't know. I was never mean to them, not once.

Anyway, it was on those holidays with the Treehuggers that I started to like Anna, not that I would ever admit it. She would play my dad's guitar and sing, and she'd laugh at herself and bite her lip and try again. She ran through the field like a kid, jumped in the creek with all her clothes on, climbed trees, and made forts with the littlest cousins. By that time, she'd stopped trying to

62

make me like her. She was always pleasant, but she didn't try to engage me anymore. I'd watch her in the firelight, the flames making her face shine while my father lay with his head in her lap. Then I wanted her to try again with me, but I knew deep down I would probably only be nice for the night, and in the morning the spell would be broken and I'd go back to being a mean girl again.

⁘

At Cheyenne's house, I water the houseplants. I gave them plant food over the weekend, but they still look sad and droopy. I take the watering can to the backyard, where I've planted my herbs. But the rosemary and lavender are turning the color of straw and the mint is turning black. The sage has weird white moldy spots and the thyme is yellow. Cheyenne's plants are all dead or dying too, except one — a poppy plant with red blooms. I don't know why this plant alone is thriving. Inspecting my herbs for pests or whatever could be hindering their growth, I find nothing and decide to cast a spell of protection for all the other plants.

In my room, I gather some dried herbs, comfrey, and patchouli and light a black candle. At my dad's house, I wasn't allowed to burn candles. This had to do with a very isolated incident in which I, as a little kid, lit a candle and let it drip its purple wax down the bathroom sink. They needed to hire a plumber to fix the sink, and after that, it was no more lit candles in the house.

Also I think Anna and my dad were a little nervous about me because Cheyenne once set fire to our apartment. They never proved it was her, but I saw her. Burning old photographs and journals on the balcony.

Anyway, Cheyenne couldn't care less if I burn candles. My cell phone chirps. It's Martin.

"Hey, what are you doing?" I ask.

"Watching TV. But I thought I'd head to the Weatherstone for a while. You want to come?"

"What's the Weatherstone?"

"Just a coffee place. You have a bike, right?"

"I do!" I say. He gives me directions and I pack up my herbs. I can always cast later. I decide to leave the candle burning for ambience. But I'm safe about it. I'm not that same old Lacy who clogged the sink with purple wax. I put the candle on a glass plate and put the plate on my dresser so that it can't catch anything on fire. I get the bike from the back and wheel it into the street.

The bike is a rusty red five-speed that my mom probably got for free. The front tire is a little bit bent, so that with every rotation, the rim brushes the frame. I steer from side to side, making swivels with my tires.

In front of me on the street, the cars and housetops are lined with snow. I pedal faster. There is snow everywhere — on the lawns of the houses, on the trees in the yards. The side streets are closed off with cones, and people stand around in crowds. There are lights and cameras. They're making a movie.

Even though it is all an illusion, it is beautiful to see. Snow in springtime. Snow in Sacramento. Once, when I was about nine, my dad and Anna and I took our bus to Arizona. In Flagstaff, we got snowed in. I had never seen snow before, and it was wild and terrific. We hunkered down in our hotel room. Anna walked to a bookstore and brought back magazines and chocolate turtles for us to read and eat in the hotel beds. In the morning we walked to a café. I pretended I was a girl from the town, one who was used to snow, and my own bed, and two parents. See them? Here they are beside me: one, two.

When I get to the Weatherstone, I can see Martin sitting outside. I prop my bike against the gate and go in and order an iced tea before going back out onto the patio to sit with him.

"Hey," I say. "Thanks for inviting me out."

"My pleasure," Martin says.

"What's that?" I point to a white frothy concoction with whipped cream in Martin's glass.

"White chocolate mocha."

"How sophisticated."

"I thank you."

I reach my finger into my iced tea and fish out a little black bug that has flown in. "Hey," I say. "Did you know that the average person eats four hundred and thirty bugs by accident every year? Random science fact."

"That is truly gross. But also kind of awesome. Probably the reason I can't lose these extra pounds." He pinches his stomach fat and we laugh.

We sit quietly for a while, watching people walk and bike by on the street. This is a nice neighborhood too, but it's no Chico. It's like, here you could be anywhere in America. But Chico has this special hum to it. You could take me anywhere in the world, drug me and confuse me, then drop me off someplace random in Chico. I totally believe that, on waking, I would know right away that I was home.

I glance at Martin. It's hard to believe he's that same kid I knew. He was so scared then, so timid.

"So, Martin, how's your dad?" It's a dangerous question. I remember how terrified Martin was of him — how he used to hide from him beneath the stairs. I hid too, but it wasn't serious for me. He only found us once, and he ignored me completely. But Martin he grabbed by the arm and shouted swearwords into his face. He dragged him upstairs to their dark apartment while Martin cried. His dad's breath had smelled like the trash cans at the park across the street.

"He died," Martin says, and he shrugs, as though talking about some unknown person, a basketball player or actor no one really liked in the first place.

"He did? How?"

"Vending machine. He really wanted that Dr Pepper." I look at Martin to see if he's joking, and he laughs a little, shaking his head. "I know it sounds crazy, but I'm actually totally serious. It fell on him." I widen my eyes, imagining it. Imagining Martin's father putting money in the machine, and pushing buttons, and waiting for the can to drop. And then, when the can refused, him kicking the machine, attacking it, until it wobbled, then fell on top of him. In horror, I laugh too — I can't help it. But Martin just shrugs again.

"Good riddance," he says. "I live with my aunt now. She's got her hands full with work, so she mostly leaves me alone. How about you? You were living with your dad in Chico?"

"Yeah," I say, and I leave it at that. I don't really feel like going into it right now.

On the street, a car door slams shut, and a girl I'm pretty sure I saw at school flips the bird to the driver as the car screeches away. Then the girl bursts into tears and takes off in the other direction.

"Doesn't she go to our school?" I ask.

"Stacia Graham. She's a freak."

"Martin," I remind him. "We're freaks too."

❖

When I get home, Cheyenne is practically in hysterics.

"You can't just leave with candles burning in your room," she says.

"I'm sorry. I put it on a plate so nothing could happen."

"Nothing could happen? Something can always happen! What if it had started a fire? They'd put arson on me so fast your head would spin."

"I'm sorry," I say again. "I didn't mean to. My room just looked so lonely. I was trying to make it look nicer."

Cheyenne breathes slowly. "You have to be punished," she says. I cringe, expecting her to hit me or lock me in the bathroom without food. Instead, her eyes dart around the room, and her gaze falls on my dad's guitar.

"No," I try to get there first, but she wins, she always wins. She snatches the guitar and holds it behind her back. "Please, that's not fair."

"You do not make the rules. I make the rules. I decide what is fair." She backs out of the room. "Stop trying to fuck this up, or else things are just going to get worse. I'm not going anywhere, and neither are you." She leaves with my guitar in hand.

At my chest, the rose necklace glows hot for a moment, then stops, and I feel a certain lightening. Like maybe the necklace was able to take away a tiny piece of my anger.

67

Even though I'd loved my bedroom at Anna's house when I was seven, I grew to resent it over the years. It felt like a trap to me, someplace I had to go when I couldn't be with my mom. And by the time I moved in full-time after she disappeared, I had grown to absolutely hate it. It felt false to me, like being inside a lie. It was painted pale yellow, and there was a patchwork comforter and stuffed tiger on the bed. They had taken down the fairy posters that had been up when I was younger, and the truth was, I wanted them back. But I wasn't about to admit it.

Anyway, I no longer believed in pretty painted walls and a bed to yourself. I believed in doing homework in the bathroom, of fleas in the bed you shared, blood on the sheets from scratching the flea bites on your back. I believed that smoking cigarettes felt good, that stealing was fun. I put my faith in the sharp tip of my mother's paring knife.

When I went to live with my dad and Anna, I brought the knife with me. But I didn't use it the first day, and I didn't use it the second day. I missed my mom, but nothing was so bad that I needed to hurt myself. The flea bites healed, and I began holding Anna to the light. They just wanted me to be a kid.

Late at night, my cell phone chirps. It's Anna.

"I'm just lying here on the couch knitting a sweater and thinking of you," she says, and I can see her there, in her gray-striped men's pajamas with sleeves that seem to swallow her hands, a blanket on her lap, and her wooden knitting needles clicking in the candlelight. "Are you doing okay?"

"I'm okay," I tell her. I don't know what else to say.

"Is Cheyenne behaving?"

"Not really."

I can hear frustration in her sigh. "I talked to your dad's lawyer. She says you need to stay with your mom, for now anyway."

"I figured."

"I'm sorry."

I stare out the doorway of my bedroom, to the wax butterflies propped above the living room mantel. They look like candles. Maybe if I could melt away the wax, live butterflies would fly up to the ceiling. I could douse my hands in sugar water and let them live on my skin. Their tongues would extend and curl like yo-yo string.

"Beltane is Friday," Anna says. "Are you doing anything?"

"Oh. I don't know."

"Do you think you could come up to visit? The Treehuggers are having a celebration. You could invite Shell and Mechelle. We could spend the night in the teepee."

"I don't know, I'll ask. She's mad at me right now, but I'll ask when she's feeling better."

Anna's voice sounds so far away over the cell phone. There's nothing she can do for me. She's in Chico, and I'm stuck here. "Lacy. Are you okay?"

I hear a thump at the sliding glass door and go to look. A dove has flown into it. Her little body is still on the back patio.

"I have to go," I say.

✛

I bring the dove into the house and lay her on the kitchen counter. She isn't dead, but she's hardly moving. In Cheyenne's closet, I find a shoe box with shoes still inside — the ones she bought in

San Miguel de Allende when she was pregnant with me. I carefully place the shoes on the top of her closet, but when I get back to the kitchen counter, the bird is dead. I pick her up, and her heart is still. I grit my teeth until they hurt and some ancient memory returns. Silver and blood. My mother at the mirror. I breathe, feeling almost faint, almost sick. I pull the bird to my chest.

With my incisors, I bite a chunk of skin from my thumb. Tears sting at my eyes as the blood pools, and I smear it on the dove's head. "Bring this creature back," I whisper aloud. "Bring her back to life." I run her to my room and open the box beneath my bed, the one with the mermaid's eye, and from it I take the bottle of silver calligraphy ink. I tear the cork stopper with my teeth and smear the bird's feathers with silver. As I chant, she begins to stir. I take the bird to the backyard and toss her toward the pool, but she flaps her wings and flies over the gate, across the neighbors' backyard. Her wings shine silver, lit by their patio light. I expect to feel relief, but I don't. I look at my hands. They are covered in blood and silver, and I feel ashamed. I have committed an act against science and nature. I should feel happy — I saved the bird, but instead I feel I've crossed some line. Dead things aren't meant to come back. Again, the necklace feels warm against the skin of my chest.

⁘

The spells were real, they had to be. I can no longer believe I may have dreamed them. My mother and I stood beneath the moon at night while that slippery thing moved in its hole. She chanted while the mild night turned stormy. She yelled at the sky and lightning lit up her face. I clutched her dress as she took out a knife and cut her fingertip. She bled into the hole. She taught me spells. Revenge spells, curses, binding spells. It is all coming back, and I hate it.

In the bathroom, I scrub at my hands, remembering the play *Macbeth*, which I saw at Shakespeare in the Park last summer. No matter how hard Lady Macbeth scrubbed, she couldn't believe the blood was ever washed from her hands. But the blood and silver come off easily, trailing in rivulets with the soapy water down the sink. I return outside, to look for the bird or just to get my bearings, and I notice something, but it takes me a moment to realize what it is. Then it dawns on me: silence. Not one croak from a single frog.

⁘

I dream that I am descending into madness. Burning cows in a field. Death beneath my feet. I stand on a sidewalk somewhere, flowers growing up through the cracks. I am an old woman. I cover my face with my hands and cry out as lightning flashes in the field. Then I am there in the field, I am tied to the tree. I open my mouth to scream, but only candle wax drips out. My chest opens, and my heart flies away. I try to catch it, but my hands are bound behind me.

When I wake up, I expect to find my heart beating wildly. But there is nothing, not even a dull thump.

CHAPTER SEVEN

My phone alarm (set to ROOSTER) crows, and the sound is excruciatingly shrill in my brain. I squeeze my eyes closed. My head won't lift off the pillow. It feels heavy and full of sand. My mouth tastes like cotton balls and socks. I drag my body to the other side of the mattress so I can snatch the phone off the floor, and my entire skull throbs. It feels like I'm growing a unicorn's horn, pressing itself through my forehead.

"Cheyenne," I call, but my throat is hoarse. And I know she sleeps like the dead.

"Mom," I try again. No answer. I fall back to sleep.

The next time I wake up, my mother is pulling off my sheets.

"Get up," she says. "You're late for school."

"I can't go to school. I'm sick."

"I'm calling bullshit."

I groan. "It's true."

She reaches out to touch my forehead. "You're burning up," she announces without any tinge of sympathy. "I thought you were faking it to get out of school."

I wish I could burn her with my fever and make her cry. But then she surprises me.

"Okay, get up. You can lie in my bed and watch TV. I'll make you soup."

❖

I drift in and out of sleep. In my dreams, there are glittering skulls like the ones in Myrna's kitchen. They laugh and taunt me. Little skeletons hang from their gruesome heads. One has a tattoo on its arm. One has yellowish eyes like a cat. I dream that I am swimming through the underwater tunnels at Bear Hole in Chico. On the creek's bottom are bloated drowned frogs, their eyes white and swollen. I try to swim away, but I get stuck in one of the crevices and can't get out. I awaken sputtering. When I sleep again, I dream of the scene in *The Wizard of Oz* when Dorothy and her friends are running through the field of red poppies. For some reason it frightens me. I try to wake myself up again, to open my eyes, but I can't.

❖

The next time I wake up, Martin is sitting on my mother's bed beside me.

"Hey, Sleeping Beauty," he is saying. "Wakey wakey, eggs and bakey."

"Hey," I say, and I struggle to sit up.

"Don't bother on my account." He waves a handout in front of me. "I brought homework," he sings.

"Thank you." I sink back into my mother's soft pillows. "That was really thoughtful of you."

He smiles, unsure of whether or not I'm joking.

"I mean it," I say. "Thank you." His smile relaxes.

"Hey, I brought you a present too." He hands me a green flowered scarf wrapped around something that jangles. I take the scarf in my hands, and the second I touch it, I know what's inside.

"Oh my gosh." I unwrap the scarf and look, confirming what I already know. "It's your bottle cap collection."

"Except for the Dr Pepper ones. I saved them, for sentimental reasons."

"You mean because of what happened to your dad?"

"Yeah. Dr Pepper is my hero."

I smile. "You're crazy. Thank you, Martin." He kisses my forehead and I close my eyes, and my dreams after that are sweet.

❖

The moon rises full and heavy outside my mother's window. Cheyenne checks her makeup in her bathroom window.

"Did you know that many brands of lipstick contain fish scales?" I ask, watching her blot at her lips. Random science fact. "It makes the lipstick shiny."

Cheyenne doesn't look too bothered by it. "Creepy," she says. "All right, I'm leaving for work. Do you need anything before I go?"

"No. Mom, come look at the moon." She turns off the bathroom light and comes to her bed and bends beside it.

"What about it?"

"It's so big. Isn't it pretty?"

"Is it full?"

"I think so."

She stays there for a moment with me, and we look at the moon together.

"Do you know the story of Artemis?"

"She was the goddess of the hunt, right?" I ask, thinking back to the block on Greek mythology I did when I was homeschooling with Anna. "Mugwort was named after her. Its botanical name is *Artemisia*. Random herbal fact."

"She was the moon goddess. She sat on a throne made of pure silver and wore a crescent moon as a crown. Some say she wore a coat made from the skin of stags she'd hunted. Once she bathed naked beneath a full moon, and she realized she was being watched by a man named Actaeon. In revenge, she threw a handful of water at him. When the water touched him, he turned into a red deer. Then she whistled for his hounds and they came. Within moments, they had shredded their poor master to bits. But that's what happens when you betray a woman of magic." She pushes my sweaty hair back from my forehead and I feel her nails lightly raking my skin. "Good night," she says softly, closing the door behind her.

After that, I can't sleep. I stare at the moon. The man in the moon, forever trapped in a howl, stares back.

⁘

In the morning, I feel well enough to make myself a garlic poultice, which I bring back to my room and lay upon my chest. It helps me breathe and soon I'm feeling even better, better enough to get up again and make myself a cup of red raspberry and peppermint tea from leaves I collected and dried in Chico. I prepare it and let it steep, and Cheyenne comes into the kitchen while I'm drinking it.

"What is that?" She frowns, sniffing the air.

"Garlic maybe? Or tea."

"My tea?"

"No, it's peppermint and red raspberry. Good for headaches and flu stuff. Do you want some?"

"Oh. No, that's okay. I just . . . the tea I make is special. I want to make sure you save it for special occasions."

"Okay," I say, trying to act like hers is a reasonable request. Special occasions. Like we have so many of those around here.

She spends the day with me, watching bad reality shows on TV from her bed. We heat up chicken noodle soup from a can and make a mess of saltines on the bedspread. Cheyenne just brushes the crumbs off wordlessly. At three, Martin comes by again with my homework. I'm feeling much better by now. I sit up and make introductions.

"Martin, do you remember my mom, Cheyenne? Cheyenne, this is Martin." She glances at me, her eyes momentarily cold as stone. She doesn't like me to call her Cheyenne, but she doesn't deserve the title Mom, even though I forget sometimes.

"We met yesterday," she says. "I let him in." If she remembers him from when he and I were kids, she doesn't let on.

"How are you, Mrs. Fin?" Martin puts his hand out to shake.

"Fine, thank you." Cheyenne lets him take her hand, but hers is limp and halting.

She stares at him, her eyebrows raised.

"Well, I guess I'd better go," Martin says. "Do you think you'll be in school tomorrow, Lacy?"

"Probably. I'm feeling a lot better."

"Oh, good. Great. Well, okay. Bye."

"Bye, Martin," I say.

After we hear the front door close, Cheyenne looks at me critically. "What is wrong with that boy? Is he retarded or something?"

"No," I say, stung. "You know he's not. Why would you say that?"

Cheyenne surveys her nails. "Most people who aren't retarded know that socks are worn on the feet."

"Well, he's not," I say, still irritated.

"I thought the gays were supposed to be fashion forward."

"*The gays,* Mom?" And then, I can't help it, I laugh. And then we're laughing together. And I called her Mom again, by accident.

⁘

The next morning when I leave for school, a little frog lies dead in the doorway. "I'm sorry," I whisper. Because I understand. When I brought the dove back to life, I stole life energy, and I stole it from this frog and the others that used to sing beneath the rosebushes. I check my hands, thinking of Lady Macbeth, but they are clean and free from blood. "I'm sorry," I whisper again, but I don't pick the frog up. I've already overstepped my bounds. I've already messed with nature.

Back at school, I feel like I'm starting all over. I feel just as displaced as I did when I first arrived. Aside from Martin, I don't have any friends. I miss Shell and Mechelle. They would like Martin. The four of us could all be friends. Martin and Mechelle could be in the school musical, and Shell and I would learn to make dry ice for effects on the stage. They could do *Sweeney Todd.* Martin could be the sinister butcher and Shell could sing about putting cats in meat pies. Standing by my locker, I smile at the thought. And I think of Zach, and I smile even wider.

I'm still grinning like an idiot when Olive Santiago passes my locker along with her crowd of worshippers. "Loser," she hisses into my face. I glare at her. She doesn't know about the demon inside me, the one who can put a curse on a girl that will make her grow old in the night, that will make her hair fall out and her skin wither like an old fruit. Olive should be careful. I have learned to keep the demon girl in check, but she is mightier than the angel on my shoulder. My mother taught me never to let anyone push me around. The Fin women are capable of anything. We can move mountains with our minds. We are dangerous and should be treated as such, with caution and respect.

Drake MacLachan, the boy with yellow eyes, slows down as he passes, and I glare at him too because he's friends with Olive.

"Hi, Lacy," he says. "You look pretty today." And then he is gone, leaving behind the smell of cloves and pepper, a strong autumn smell. "Why say fall when you can say autumn instead?" my mother used to say. I spin to watch him as he walks away, and he turns back, one time, and winks at me. *He's probably a total jerk*, I am thinking, but I feel the flurry of wings in my chest.

✥

I am a Gemini, which means, astrologically speaking, there are two sides to me. I am charming and lively; I am superficial and cunning. Or so they say. I am the good twin and the bad twin all rolled up into one. Don't blame me, blame my evil twin. You won't have to look hard to find her.

I believe in ghosts and voodoo and the planets that rule us. The moon affects the tides, so why shouldn't the stars shape our destiny? Sun signs, moon signs, ruling planets. My starstone is moss agate. My ruling planet is Mercury. It all sounds so beautiful and mysterious to me.

Anna too believes in astrology, and she always buys those little plum-colored horoscope scrolls in the supermarket. But I don't waste my money on those things. I could see myself, in some other life, poring through them, looking for meaning. Little orphan girl. Poor sad little me.

I am what they say about Gemini, though. Two-sided. There is the me I long to be all the time, the one that feels like me, and then there is this other person who is more like my mother, and she is dismal, ugly, and dark. Filled to the brim with tears and muck. Dark, churning inside, like I have swallowed enough quarts of motor oil to fill me. This is the twin, the stranger. She is coming back, invasive and sick. I am afraid she will push the good twin out.

✤

On the phone, Anna sounds so far away. She puts Mr. Murm on to murm. "Can you hear him?" she asks, and I lie, "Yes."

"Did you talk to Cheyenne about Beltane?"

"Yes," I say, my body heavy with the lies. "She told me it's not a good time."

I do want to go up to Chico for Beltane. I do want to sleep in the teepee, to see Shell and Mechelle and the Treehuggers, who I miss like crazy. I want to visit my dad's grave, bring him snapdragons, his favorite flower. But I don't want to ask Cheyenne for it. She'll say no, and then she'll be taking something away from me. I can't stand for her to take away any more.

✤

In an effort to be the good Gemini twin, I have decided to stop eating meat. Martin and I sit at school with our lunches under the gray pine tree. Martin is on a "sexy foods diet" this week; his lunch consists of canned asparagus and oysters lifted from Rite Aid, along with a mango. My lunch is carrot sticks and tofu puffs, which are left over from the dinner I made myself last night.

"Yum," I say, squeezing a cold tofu puff between my fingers. "Leftover deep-fried bean curd."

"Ooh, yummy," Martin says. "What is bean curd made out of anyway?"

"Kittens," I say.

"Hitler's brain," he counters. "Remind me why you're a sudden vegetarian?"

"Because I looove animals," I say, and while it's true, we both know this isn't the reason.

I am smooshing the puff and letting it pop back to its regular form, when Olive and her cronies walk by. Chad Vanner is trying to jump onto Olive's back and ride her piggyback, and Olive laughs and turns and snaps her gum in his face. Suddenly, they are totally kissing, all over each other, and right next to where Martin and I are sitting. It is gross. I don't even understand how they can breathe. This is something I have wondered about kissing, and it kind of freaks me out. How do you catch your breath when there's someone right there sucking it all out? I don't know and I don't want to know. Well, okay, I kind of want to know.

Yeah, it's true, sweet sixteen and never been kissed. I can't explain it. It just hasn't happened. I've been friends with a lot of boys, but it's just never come to that. Maybe Zach and I would have kissed by now if I hadn't had to move to Sacramento. But let's face it, probably not.

I am making a face of disgust to show Martin how ostentatious I think the snotty kids are, and suddenly I feel a hot breath in my left ear. "Fin," a voice says, "I want to do things to you."

"Ew!" I say as I turn and see Drake MacLachan straightening out to his full height beside me. His silhouette is black against the sun. Then he moves away and the sunlight hits his face and he winks. "Pervert!" I shout after him.

"Uh-oh. What was that about?" Martin asks.

"I don't know." I really don't. My skin crawls, but not with disgust. With pleasure, and something else besides.

⬧

At home, Cheyenne makes me a cup of tea and it isn't even a special occasion.

"What kind of tea is this?" I ask her.

"It comes from Europe. It's supposed to support well-being and ease." It does. It makes me tired, but it does something else, something helpful. It tastes so good and makes me feel so relaxed that I can't say no when she offers it to me. I hold the warm cup in my cold hands. It is a warm afternoon, a premonition of the hot Sacramento summer to come. One day it is chilly, the next it is sweltering, but my hands and feet are always cold. I lie down beside her on the couch and press my cold feet into her calves. "You can have your guitar back if you want," she says, and I mumble thanks, grateful but unable to express it. Absentmindedly, she rubs my leg and I feel it, that current that runs between us. Her eyes are slits as she stares out the window onto the hot street. I shiver once, and then I am asleep.

CHAPTER EIGHT

I am doing nothing for Beltane. No maypole, no flowers, no altar of pomegranates and cherries. I know that Anna is probably driving to the Treehuggers' house right now. They will raise a maypole and dance beneath it. They will write poems to the earth and send them down the creek in paper boats. They'll make daisy chains and wear them in their hair. And when the sun goes down, they'll burn the maypole ribbons in a bonfire, and the Treehuggers will give a private concert. And I'll be here, alone in my room with my dad's guitar, which I don't even know how to play.

✤

On the second Saturday of every month, Sacramento has an art walk downtown. I don't remember Cheyenne ever taking me in the past, but she swears she has.

"You remember," she informs me in the car. "Someone gave you a balloon, and you let it go and it blew away. You wouldn't stop crying. You made such a scene that a little boy gave you his to shut you up."

"How old was I?" I ask.

"Who knows. Three maybe? It was during your impossible stage."

I don't know how she expects me to remember an art walk I went to when I was three, but I don't say anything as my necklace warms my chest and she finds a parking spot and expertly parallel parks.

Dressed in her silk mandarin top, judo pants, and San Miguel de Allende shoes, she looks elegantly uncomfortable this hot Sacramento day. But Cheyenne doesn't even break a sweat. We wander into the galleries, looking at altered birdhouses and wire art. Baby heads on plaster and what look like paintings but are really clusters of colored feathers. Cheyenne turns up her nose at the free wine, even though she drinks at home. "That swill," she says, plucking a grape between her fingertips and popping it into her mouth. "I guess it's fine for most people. We Fins don't waste our spit."

She narrows her eyes, scanning the room for an artist she knows. When she finds him, she ditches me beside the food table and moves to the back of the room, through the crowds of people, like she's being swept up in a cool breeze.

I take a handful of grapes and cheese crackers outside to where a band is playing U2 cover songs to a crowd of mildly interested people. A little girl lets go of her balloon, but she doesn't cry as it soars up into the cloudless evening sky, a smear of red against the purple lit-up night. Instead, she laughs and points.

When Cheyenne comes back out, she is angry. "Let's go," she says, breezing past me, and I hop from my seat and struggle to keep up. But on the way to the car, she stops. An attractive man with crazy-white teeth and dimples stands in front of one of the galleries, smiling at her. I watch as Cheyenne's mask of anger transforms instantly to radiance.

"Hello," she says. "Have we met?"

"I don't think so," he says, stammering a little. "Maybe in my dreams."

Oh my God, it is just so gross I could throw up, and Cheyenne clearly thinks so too, as her smile turns immediately to scorn. But just then, a woman comes out of the gallery and makes a beeline for us, and she loops her arm through the cheesy man's arm, and Cheyenne smiles again, enjoying the woman's discomfort.

"Let's go," the woman says.

"Um, sure, um, maybe I'll see you around sometime?"

"I hope so." Cheyenne grins and tilts her head to the side. The woman pouts as she looks past my mother, then she begins pulling at the man's arm. But he stands, mute as stone, nodding like a happy clown. My mother beams. I have heard men call her head gamer. I have heard men call her cock tease. She is a witchy woman, Cheyenne. Not one of us stands a chance.

⋇

That night my cell phone chirps; it is a number I don't know. I pick up on the third ring.

"Fin," a familiar voice says. "What are you wearing?"

My heart catches in my throat. "Drake MacLachan, you are disgusting."

He laughs. "I'm only playing."

"Do you want something?"

"I just wanted to hear your voice."

"How did you even get my phone number?"

"I have my ways."

I bite my lip, unsure what to say. Why isn't there a manual on what to do when a rude boy at the new school where you're considered a freak seems to like you? Although he is definitely good-looking, in a kind of scary catlike way.

"I just think you're really pretty. And you seem interesting. I've never met anyone like you before."

"Like me? But you don't even know me."

"I know, but I would like to. The other girls at school, Olive and the rest of them, they're immature. They just care about makeup and partying. You seem different. You care about things that are important."

"I guess I do."

"You do. I can tell just by looking at you. Hey, do you want to go to San Francisco with me some weekend? We could take the train. I'll take you to City Lights bookstore where the Beats used to read their poetry, and I can show you where the Grateful Dead and Janis Joplin used to live."

"I don't . . . know if I'm allowed."

"I know it sounds crazy, but it would be fun. We could get to know each other in that beautiful city. Think about it."

"Okay," I say after a pause. "I'll think about it." But my insides are all trembly and I feel a surge of excitement thinking of the two of us on the train together. It sounds romantic, like an old movie. I do want to go to San Francisco with him. I'll find a way.

"Good night, Lacy Fin. Sweet dreams."

"Night," I say, and another little shudder of pleasure goes through me as I close the phone.

❖

After Cheyenne goes to bed, I walk outside to my garden. The planets are bright and piercing in the night sky. A thimbleful of a neutron star would weigh over one hundred million tons. Random science fact.

When I was little and couldn't fall asleep, my dad always took me outside to watch the stars. When I was with him and Anna, I was usually homesick for my mom. I would be in tears and gulping down sobs, my legs would hurt, and he'd lift me from my bed and carry me outside.

"Don't wish on the first star you see," he would whisper in the gathering dark. "It's a planet. If you want your wish to come true, wait until the real stars come out. There," he would say, pointing toward a small flickering light. "There." He would point, and I'd trace his movements with my fingertips across the sky.

My dad was tall and scruffy, with a little bit of a beard and eyebrows that shot into a million different directions. He always wore a Columbia hat he'd bought at REI. Anna said he wore it because he was self-conscious about his receding hairline. She said people gave him a hard time about it, and I didn't need her to clarify which people.

I know he wasn't perfect, but I loved him more than anyone. I remember splashing in the water while he stood by at Alligator Hole. He was blowing bubbles from a plastic jug, and I was running through the water ankle-deep trying to catch them. There were dragonflies and damselflies everywhere, and later, cold, I snuggled into his arms and he said, "This is my favorite moment. This moment has wings, can you see that?"

The birds came to his funeral. Owls and egrets, hawks and quail and mourning doves. They flew in from the clouds, perching in the oak and Japanese zelkova trees. People put up their umbrellas even though there was no rain. The birds had come to grieve for my dad, the man who had once rescued a pigeon from a hawk, who had carried the pigeon home in his arms while the hawk cried out angrily above them. Birds landed on the weeping angel of grief. The wings of the statue seemed to flutter in the cool winter air. The pastor called the grave his final resting place, and I cried into Anna's lap. The birds looked on, their black eyes like river stones, and I wondered even then if Cheyenne was watching, somehow, from some undetected place.

CHAPTER NINE

In English class, we're talking about *The Scarlet Letter*, which I already read last year. I take out a piece of paper like I'm taking notes, but instead I write *DRAKE* with each of the letters right on top of another so that anyone who looks at the paper would not be able to read it. Then I write *LACY* over the letters. Our names overlapping like this look like a birdcage. I write the names again, but in lowercase. Then I write *LACY MACLACHAN*, and it looks like a tree in front of mountains. Or a stained-glass window. It all looks really pretty, if you look at it the right way.

"Lacy?" Mrs. Kesey is saying.

"What?" Everyone laughs.

"I'll repeat the question. Why was Pearl upset when she first saw her mother without the *A*?"

"Um, because she was used to it?"

"Okay. Can anyone expand on that?"

I look at Drake. He winks at me and I smile back. Then I go back to my notes. In cursive, our names look like a turtle on its side.

❖

After school, I ride my bike to the American River Bike Trail and sit beside the river to harvest wild fennel and California mugwort, both of which can be dried for tea. I'm also low on my plantain tincture, so I grab batches of plantain leaf too. It grows in clumps like a weed but is a natural remedy for stings and wounds and even acne. The Native Americans called it life medicine because it can be used for so many things.

The sun is still high in the sky — every day another reminder that summer is coming. From down the river, I hear high-pitched voices, and soon a group of children appears wearing rain boots and tie-dye shirts and matching sun hats of various bright colors — pink, yellow, blue, green, purple. Their teacher carries an African basket like the one Anna carries to the farmers market.

For a single moment, I want to be one of those children, stomping through the mud in my rain boots, finding clovers and pretty leaves for my teacher to put in her basket. Once they have passed me, I feel supremely alone. The teacher had nodded her head at me, and her smile had seemed so quiet and shy. Maybe she was the kind of person who could only stand to be around little kids. Maybe she was terrified by the largeness of teenagers and grown-ups.

The leaves rustle in the trees, and I close my eyes to listen. They sound dry, like autumn leaves cracking against one another, but they are green against the blue sky. I hear a sound behind me, and the hairs on the back of my neck stand up. It is Drake MacLachan, walking his own bike behind me.

"What are you doing here?" I ask, scowling. "Did you follow me?"

"Don't flatter yourself," he says. But then he kneels beside me. "Yeah," he admits. "What are you doing?"

"I'm collecting these herbs. Look, this is Queen Anne's lace. See the little red flower in all the white? It's supposed to represent a drop of Queen Anne's blood from where she pricked her finger while making lace. Random herbal fact."

"Cool. How did you learn all this?"

"Books mostly. I have a collection of old books I bought with my stepmom. We try to learn everything. 'The more you learn, the more power you have over your life.' That's what she says. So what do you want, anyway?" I am trying to sound cool but I sound like a little girl instead.

He looks into my eyes and takes my hand. "I want you."

I snap my hand away. "Why?"

"What do you mean, why?" He looks so genuine, so true. "You're beautiful. And you're fascinating."

"Me?" I laugh and turn away, his eyes so golden, his gaze so intense. "I'm not fascinating."

"You are, though. Like a girl in a poem."

I laugh again, a snorting type sound from my nose, but he won't let me dismiss him. He takes my hand again. "Come sit with me," he says. Then he pulls me toward the river, away from the bikes, and he's pulling me and we laugh. Not all that different from the little kids on the path. I picture us in tie-dye and rainbow hats. He's only a boy. He makes me nervous, but he's really just a boy. I think about a movie I watched about a bunch of boys at summer camp. Not that long ago, Drake was the age of those boys. Telling poop jokes and making fart noises with his armpits.

He pulls me down and we sit beside the river. He takes a book from his back pocket. "Rimbaud," he says, indicating the book.

"Rambo? That boxer guy?"

Drake laughs and I immediately feel stupid. "Rambo was an army guy played by Sylvester Stallone, who also played a boxer in *Rocky*. Rimbaud is a poet." He shows me the cover before opening the book and beginning to read. " 'I laughed at the blond waterfall that tousled through the pines: on the silver summit I recognized the goddess. Then, one by one, I lifted up her veils. I wrapped her up in her gathered veils, and I felt a little her immense body.' "

"It's beautiful," I say, but I bite my lip and feel heat rise to my cheeks. It is partly the language of the poem, which somehow makes me feel exposed, like those dreams where you're at school with only underwear on. Also, I'm still embarrassed about the whole Rambo thing.

"He must have written it about someone just like you."

It's cheesy, I know. But no one has ever looked at me this way before. I carefully pluck a blade of grass from its sheath and break the delicate green leaf of grass with my thumbnail. I form perfect wet green squares that rest on my fingertip.

"You're a little dangerous, aren't you?" Drake says, and I feel like he's looking right into my soul. "I like danger." I imagine myself the way I must seem to him at school when I regard Olive and her friends with a cold stare. Like a fierce bird with stony eyes, or an animal with a snarl and sharp teeth. I give him a brief smile. He tells me he'll come to my house at midnight.

❖

All night I lie awake listening for the light tap of pebbles on my window. Finally, long after midnight, I hear a car door slam and the sound of footsteps on the sidewalk outside. And then the sound I'm waiting for. Click. Click. Pebbles on the glass. Before pushing off the covers, I revel for a moment. I am the kind of girl who draws men to her bedroom window in the middle of the night. A girl from a poem. I am that girl.

I open my window and climb through it. I could just as easily go out through the front door, but this seems more glamorous, more romantic. Of course, it's a one-story house, but my window is raised, level with the front porch. I step onto the edge of the fence and hop down into the wet grass at his feet. Drake stands above me, his body silhouetted against the moonlight. He reaches out his hand and I take it. We are a music video under the moon.

"I stole my parents' car to get here," he tells me, and it seems bad and dangerous and awesome.

"Where do you want to go?" I ask.

"I just want to be with you."

We cross the street on foot and walk several blocks to the baseball field hand in hand. He holds a sound dock the shape of a cube under his arm. The moon is low in the purple sky, and the song he plays is "Moondance" by Van Morrison, and he reaches out his hand for me again and we dance. My cheek is against his chest and he smells like cloves. He feels so strong and I feel fragile in his arms. *I will love you forever*, some deep part of me whispers to my brain, but I would never say it aloud. I rest my head against his chest and picture myself saying those words, and I picture the way he would look at me, eyes wide and nervous, and he might leap like a gazelle back to my house, and by the time I got back, he would be gone in his parents' car, disappearing into the moonlit night. So instead I say, "This is nice." And he puts his hands on the sides of my face and he tilts my face up, and then we are going to kiss. And I want to freeze in this moment. My insides are all trilly and his face is so close to mine. And the kiss is so soft and his lips are so soft, and my underwear is getting wet. His hands are in my hair and he is kissing my neck, and then he takes a step away. And I am glad, because for a moment there, I thought this might be going too fast. But Drake is an old soul, the kind of person who reads poetry, who sneaks out in the night to play music for a girl, to hold her close in intimacy and dance.

After a while, he walks me home.

✜

At school, Drake stands holding open the door to English class.

"Mademoiselle," he says. I glide past him, feeling like a princess or a debutante. In black fairy dress and black leggings, I feel beautiful, and not because I look like my mother. "You're a little dangerous," he had said. It's like he sees something true inside me.

"Thank you," I say, and he smiles at me, sending the trillies back into my chest. I remember the kisses from last night, the one on my lips and the one on my neck. He bends down to whisper in my ear. "Tonight?" he asks. I suck in my bottom lip and smile and nod. Tonight again. I am the luckiest girl in the school.

✜

After lunch when I come out of the stall of the girls' room, Stacia Graham is standing at the mirror. She is taller than most of the boys, and she wears short hair and red lips like a valentine. The kids at school all say she's a slut, but everyone's afraid of her. She looks like she could slaughter you with a glance, like she could slice you to pieces with her chipped blue fingernails.

I quickly wash my hands and try to duck past her, but she steps in front of me. She maneuvers her neck in such a way that we are eye to eye, even though she is so much taller than me.

"Fin," she says. "I notice Drake's sniffing after you." She waits to let me speak, but I have nothing to say, so I let her continue. "He's a total jerk. I'm just letting you know."

"Okay," I say. "Thanks." I duck my head, and this time she lets me pass her.

⁙

He's waiting for me by my bike after school, where he's parked illegally in the red and is leaning against his parents' Prius. A couple of his guy friends are standing there too. "There she is," he says, and his eyes fill with warmth. They usually still look cold to me, like cat eyes, but just now, in the parking lot next to the bike rack and his friends, they are gold and amber and full of something beautiful.

"Hi," I say, shy because of his friends, but I reach my hand out and he takes it.

"Hi," he says, pulling me closer. His friends laugh and Drake smiles. "Ignore those assholes," he says, and he kisses me right there in front of his friends and God and everyone. "Tonight," he murmurs against my cheek, and then he releases me and I float away in the direction of home before I remember I need to go back for my bike.

CHAPTER TEN

When I get home from school, Cheyenne is still in bed. I know she doesn't get out of bed on rainy days; those days she spends in her pajamas, her head beneath her pillow. But today is as warm and clear as any spring day in Sacramento, and I know she has to get to work by five.

In the kitchen, I make her a cup of dandelion root tea, good for energy and endurance, and bring it to her.

"Cheyenne," I say, pulling on her brocade sleeve. "It's past three. You need to get up."

"Why?" she drawls, smacking her lips like a sleepy child and putting her hand over her eyes.

"You have work. You can't just lie in bed all day."

"Mmmm. You're no fun. Come on, lie down, let's go to sleep."

"Cheyenne, I'm not tired. I have homework. It's like three thirty." But looking at her, all warm and snug beneath her Egyptian cotton sheets, I think how nice it would be to take a break from the rest of the day, to let the homework rot in its pile, to collapse into the soft warm sleep of a child. I could still be up by the time Drake gets here. In fact, if I go to bed now, I'll be more rested for the evening.

But what am I thinking? I can't do that. I have a history paper to write, three to five pages on the French and Indian War due tomorrow, not to mention algebra and French. Pataud the *chien* awaits. *J'attends, tu attends, il/elle/on attend, nous attendons, vous attendez, ils/ells attendent.*

I have to dig beneath some magazines and newspapers to find the phone. I dial the number for the bar Cheyenne works at. "I'm calling in sick for my mother," I tell them. But I know how this goes. She probably won't be going back there again.

❖

Right before my mom disappeared, we'd started getting along. By then I'd chopped off all my hair and had started wearing eyeliner. I'd started smoking cigarettes and stealing and cutting class. I was thirteen. Maybe it all made her think of me as a grown-up. She talked to me like one, and I liked it. I liked that she was talking to me at all. "We are rare birds with sharp teeth and gilded wings," she would tell me. "We soar above the roofs and treetops, shooting through clouds and tickling the moon. The stars are our nightclubs where we dress in silver bangles and eat men whole before spitting them out. People tell us we have our heads in the clouds and we laugh, ferociously, baring our teeth. We don't much like to be pulled down to earth."

We were going to New York, she told me. We would get a little apartment in the Village, become bohemian artists; we'd lock our doors and let no one inside. We'd let vines grow up to cover the windows so no one could see in. From there we'd go to Paris, where we'd carry baguettes home from the market, speaking French to the street artists as we walked along the Seine.

"Just you and me," she told me. "My blood is in you. Our bones are intertwined." And I believed her. I packed my bag. I was ready to leave everyone behind.

But then she was sleeping all the time — nothing new there until she started throwing up as well. I thought she was sick. That was when I learned to make tea myself — I made it for her and brought it to her cluttered bedside in thick clay mugs we'd found at a park fair for cheap: 70% CLEARANCE. She drank the tea, but it made her cry. I didn't know why. I drank the same tea, and it didn't make me sad at all. It made me think of my dad, and that made me happy.

And then I started noticing something. A bulge at her navel. Right where her belly button was. My always skinny mother. She didn't like me to touch her. And I knew. Something was going to come between us and we would never be the same. And I knew then that I would stop at nothing to keep it from happening. After all, I was my mother's daughter.

❖

My dad got his guitar from his grandmother. It's very old, and the backs and sides are made of Brazilian rosewood. He used to play it when we were camping out, and Anna would beat her little djembe drum. He said he wasn't a very good player, and maybe he wasn't. But he was good enough that the Treehuggers asked him to be in their band. He said no. At the time, he was married to my mom.

The Treehuggers' band is actually called Tree Hugging Hypocrisy, and even though he wasn't an official member, my dad was like their mascot. He'd go to a lot of their shows dressed up in a chicken suit, and he'd dance. Anna says the first time they met, he was dressed in his chicken suit. She went up behind him and tapped him on the shoulder, and he jumped, and she said, "Don't be alarmed. I'm a vegetarian."

I wish I knew how to play. I take the guitar on my lap and strum a few chords. I know A, D, E, C, and G. I can play "Leaving on a Jet Plane" and "This Land Is Your Land." I can fingerpick "Happy Birthday." There are pearl inlays on the fret board. He held it so gently in his large hands.

⁂

I make another cup of dandelion root tea and bring it to my mother in her room. I don't want to disturb her, but as I set the cup on her nightstand, she reaches out from under her covers and grabs my wrist.

"Oh," I say, jumping. "I didn't know you were awake."

"I am always awake," she says in her cryptic way. I know she isn't always awake. It's just one of the weird things she likes to say. "So" — she pulls me so that I'm sitting beside her on the bed — "how's school going?"

"It's fine," I say, surprised that she's taking an interest.

"Met any real boys yet?"

"A couple," I say, missing the slam to Martin, thinking only of Drake.

"Darling." She sits up and leans against a pillow, then takes a sip of the tea I gave her. I watch to see if it makes her sleepy and weird, like it does me, but it doesn't seem to have an effect. Then again, she was already sleepy and weird. "I hope you don't make the same mistakes I made."

"Like what?" I am already skeptical.

"I got married too young. I married the wrong man. Be cool. Stay in school. Don't lose your virginity to the first guy willing to hop in the sack with you."

"Mom!" I am mortified. I can't believe she is saying this to me.

"What? I'm just saying you should be careful. Men aren't always what they seem."

"Like Dad?" I ask only because I sense that she's beating around the bush, and I want her to get to the point.

"Oh, I know you loved your father. And he was a good man, for the most part. But there are things about him you don't know."

"Please don't tell me this," I plead, and I shake my head slowly. I want to get up, walk away, but this is the kind of strange hypnotic power she has over me.

"Well, I think it's only fair for you to know. He and I, we are the monsters who made you. It's our blood coursing through you. You deserve to know what you are."

"None of us are monsters." I look down at her comforter and tears fall straight from my eyeballs; they don't stream down my face at all. "My dad was not a monster."

"I see." She sounds smug and mean. "But you think I am one."

"That's not what I meant." Now the tears pool in my eyes as I look at her, but her expression is as cold as the stone goddess in front of Myrna's shop. "Please."

"Your father was not the angel you think he was. He was abusive. He broke walls with his bare fists. Once he broke down the bathroom door to get in at me. I was hiding from him in there. From his rage."

"No."

"Darling," she says, and her voice softens. "I'm only telling you this because I want you to be careful. I don't want you to be weak like I was. Now stop crying and harden your heart." She smiles. "You are Lacy Fin. You are a fierce bird; you eat men whole. You don't let anyone push you around. Remember."

I nod my head, only because I can't wait to get out of her room. Finally she lets me go. She sinks back down under her covers, like a sea monster returning to her cave.

✥

I try to write my history paper, but my mind keeps returning to the image of my dad breaking down the door. He did have a temper. Especially when it came to Cheyenne. I remember what felt like nightly rages at his house when I was very little, maybe six or seven. On the weekends I was with him, my mother would call for me on the phone, then ask to talk to him. He would already look angry as I passed him the phone. He'd take it reluctantly, narrowing his eyes as he said, "Hello?"

Then he'd be shouting into the phone, and I would cry behind a chair in the living room. Anna would continue knitting with a dark look over her face and ultimately he would hang up while Cheyenne was still talking. Then he'd pick up the phone again and slam it. Once, sometimes twice. Afterward he would apologize to me. He and I would go out for ice cream and he'd tell me he had a temper. He'd tell me my mother made him mad sometimes. I just remember licking at my pralines 'n' cream and feeling mostly sorry for myself. I think I was too young back then for my life.

✥

Click. Click. The pebbles on the glass. I stretch and rise from my sheets. My face reflects back at me from the window, and beyond it, dark street, bright beautiful boy. I wave to let him know I've heard. I climb out the window and drop from the fence to the grass below. Drake reaches for me and lifts me to my feet. Without a word, we head for the field.

This time he has brought a blanket and a bottle of white wine. He unscrews the top and pours the wine into Dixie cups and holds one out to me. I hesitate before taking the cup. Anna wouldn't do it. She is good and pure. My mother would drink it down in one gulp. Or maybe she wouldn't: "We Fins wouldn't waste our spit." So what? I am my own person. I drink it down.

It burns like stars ripping my throat apart and my body feels hot and sick. Drake is watching me. "Whoa," he says. "Is it good? Do you want some more?"

"Sure," I say. "Why not?" He fills my cup and I take a sip.

"Cheers," Drake says, and he holds out his cup. I touch mine to his, and then I drink this cup too. It isn't very good. It tastes like feet. I set the cup beside me on the grass like it's a precious thing, not a paper cup of cheap wine from a bottle with a screw top. He sets his cup down too and leans into me, and I want to pause again, to feel the moment before the kiss, but he is too fast and his lips are on mine before I can take a breath.

His mouth is huge against mine, almost humorous. Hot giant mouth. I pull away to catch my breath, but he follows me and then he is on top of me. I don't mind that. His body pressing mine against the earth. But it's too fast. I like him on top of me, but I want it to stop there. A few kisses like this. And then I want us to recite fairy tales or go to sleep or something. Instead, he reaches up my shirt and it isn't what I want, and his fingers are kind of hard like rubber erasers and they poke and grope at me. "Stop," I say, but his mouth is covering mine and his hand is reaching into my pants. His fingers find their way into my underwear and then they are inside me. I gasp and push him off me.

He laughs, a cool metallic laugh. "Come on, Lacy," he says. "Don't tell me you're a prick tease." He pushes me back with his body, and his fingers reach farther inside, stretching me open. Above me the moon hides behind branches of a tree. And the branches are crisscrossed above me like a spiderweb, like a thatched roof, like a cage. A tear runs down my cheek. He reaches for the button on his jeans and I scurry out from under him, backward, until my back is against the trunk of a tree.

I put my head against my knees and cry. My necklace glows warm and I hold it in my hand.

Drake scoffs. "Pathetic," I hear him say. "I should have known. You're not different. You're not dangerous. You're pathetic. Fucking virgins, man. These head games you all play. Call me when you're ready to cut the shit." He stands and starts to walk away, leaving me rolled up like a ball, like a pile of trash.

"Wait," I say, and he turns back to look at me. "Don't be mad," I plead. "I just wasn't ready." I sound like a baby. "I like you. I wasn't trying to play with your head."

He scoffs again. "Right. Like you didn't know what you were doing. Strutting around school in your Catwoman outfits, acting like you think you're better than everyone else. But you're nothing, nothing but a little bitch. A waste of time." He walks away, and I cry into my knees. Forget him; he's an asshole. Only what if he's right? Head games, cock tease, I've heard all this stuff before. I've heard men scream it about my mother, so loudly their voices shook the walls. And I know my mother dresses provocatively. Is that what I look like in the clothes Myrna made? An easy girl, a slut? I thought I was good, but what if it turns out I'm just as confused and damaged as she is?

✤

I am capable of bad things. I know that. Moved by jealousy, I am capable of evil. When I was little, I wanted to go to Paris. I wanted my mother to myself, and I did bad things to make that happen. In the end, it didn't even matter; she left me all alone. I wish I were a robot, incapable of emotion. The best thing would be to not let myself feel anything at all.

✤

The next day, I dress for school in my old Chico clothes: a science camp T-shirt and the comfy sweats I used to wear to bed. In the hallway, Stacia Graham looks at me, and her eyes are questioning. Obviously, he hurt her too. I try to smile at her, but I think it comes out a frown.

Drake is already in English when I get there. I slide into my seat and glare at him, hoping he can feel my hatred through the back of his head. Instead, he leans over and says something to his friend Jacob, and Jacob looks at me and snorts a laugh. We hold each other's gaze, and after a minute, Jacob opens his eyes wide and gapes at me, mocking. Drake peers at me sideways and then drops his head to his desk, cracking up. My necklace radiates its heat. I hate him. He is the world's biggest asshole and I hate him.

I open my binder and find a blank piece of paper. On it I draw a picture of Drake, only he's dismembered and blood is dripping from his eyes. I write the words without thinking: *You're treating girls like they're nothing but dirt. And now for that you too must hurt. As I cast this simple spell, I bind you to your own dark hell.*

When I'm done writing, I almost laugh. Stupid laughable girl, casting made-up spells to feel some sort of power. Drake was right. I am nothing, nothing but a little bitch. While Ms. Kesey lectures, I tear the paper into tiny strips, and when the bell rings, I deposit them in the trash can on my way out the door.

CHAPTER ELEVEN

Crossing through the field to get home, I see Stacia Graham standing by the parking lot. When she sees me coming, she starts toward me.

"Hey," I say.

"I'm sorry," she says. "I told you Drake's an asshole, but you didn't listen."

"No, I know," I say. "You were right."

"Drake is telling people you slept with him. Just so you know." She drops her gaze and starts plucking at her fingernails. She looks almost like a little kid.

"What a dick. I take it he did the same thing to you?"

She glances back up and her eyes are wet. "Yeah. I really wanted him to like me. I almost went all the way with him. But I decided I wasn't ready. The next day at school I tried to apologize, but by then he'd already told everyone I was a slut." She sits on the pavement and picks up a pebble. She rolls it around between her fingertips. "He'll probably say that about you too."

I sit quietly for a minute, anger boiling inside me. "We shouldn't be the ones apologizing," I finally say. "Anyway, who cares what all the kids at school think?" Stacia doesn't say anything. We both know that we both care. "What a dick."

"Did he tell you he was going to take you to San Francisco? And recite you a poem by Rimbaud? That poem isn't even about a girl, it's about the summer dawn. Sleazeball."

I sit down on the pavement beside her. "So I guess he'll just keep tormenting girls."

"I'm sure we weren't the first ones."

I am silent for a minute, picturing the school halls filled with girls who snuck out in the night with Drake, who drank his cheap wine under a thatched sky and woke up the next morning with her pride or virginity gone, with quiet stares and whispers in the hallways. I imagine an army of girls, faceless and silent, roaming the halls like zombies in an old movie.

"We have to stop him," I say.

Stacia snorts. "Right. I tried to stop you."

"Is anyone at your house?" I ask.

"No, my parents are at work."

"Can we go there?" Stacia shrugs and we cross back through the field toward Sac State.

❖

Spells, old spells, rearrange themselves in my head. They come unbidden, dangerous and real. A little bit scary. Things my mother taught me, when I was so little. My little brain had no choice but to hold them, to stow them away. Now they come back, but they are jumbled; I'm not sure how to piece them together. Something tells me it doesn't matter, that the magic will find its way.

I follow Stacia to one of the condominium complexes near the college. We enter the back porch through the carport. Stacia uses her key to unlock the sliding glass door.

The room we walk into is adjacent to the kitchen. There is a bowl of limes on the counter and a binding spell makes its way from the jumble to the tip of my brain. It doesn't scare me. It makes me feel powerful. "Can we use one of these limes?" I ask and Stacia nods. "Where are your knives?" She opens a drawer without asking why and hands me a sharp paring knife. I cut the lime into quarters, leaving each quarter attached to the peel. "You don't have a picture of Drake, do you?" I ask.

"I have last year's yearbook."

"Can we cut his picture out?"

"Like I care." Stacia shrugs.

"Okay. I need some string, a piece of paper, and a nail too," I say, and Stacia raises her eyebrows at me, but she goes. When she comes back with everything, I find Drake's student picture in the yearbook and tear it out. He looks so smug with his cat eyes. I don't know how I ever thought he was cute. He looks like a boy who could hurt a girl. His eyes so smug and mean. I wrap the string tightly around the picture, concealing first his eyes, then his mouth.

Next I tear the piece of blank computer paper in half. One piece I put between two halves of the lime, and the other I set on the counter. I drive the nail through the lime, and I remember. I've done this spell before. Against my mother. So that she couldn't hurt Anna and my dad. Well, good. I'm glad I did that. I ask Stacia for a jar.

"You're a trip, Fin," Stacia says, rummaging under the sink and coming up with an old peanut butter container. "Will this work as a jar?"

"It's supposed to be glass, but this is better than nothing." I drop the lime and the wrapped picture from the yearbook into the jar. "Now we write Drake's name on this half of the paper, set it on fire, and let the ash fall into the jar." This time Stacia doesn't even raise her eyebrows as she finds a Sharpie, a lighter, and a metal bowl. She writes *Drake MacLachan* in dark bold print, then crumples the paper and lights it on fire. We watch as the flame moves from one edge of the crumpled ball toward the top, fanning higher until it is going to burn Stacia's finger, and when she drops it into the metal bowl, I realize she has had practice lighting things on fire. Smoke billows out and bits of glowing ember consume the creases of the paper like growing things, red mushrooms in a sped-up video. Stacia dumps the ash into the peanut butter container.

"Now what?" she asks.

"Tonight we go to the school and bury it," I tell her.

❖

The school looks much different at night, when all the lights are turned out. It looks like an institution, a spooky place that might capture a girl's soul. With our flashlights, we head to the cherry tree, the one where Olive and Drake and their friends hang out. If it were daytime, you would be able to see the bright pink blossoms, so pretty you know such a color couldn't exist in a world without magic. We drop to our knees, and I feel the coolness of the earth through my sweatpants. I find a rock with a sharp edge and begin to dig, and when I abandon the rock, I use my strong gardener hands to pull the dirt in clumps. I try not to think of my father. Of all that death beneath the soil.

Stacia joins me in digging. "What is this supposed to do?" she asks for the first time.

"It's a binding spell. It's supposed to keep him from hurting other people," I tell her. "It's black magic, which I never use." I catch myself in my own accidental lie. I never *used* to use black magic. But resurrection spells are black magic too. It's my fault all those frogs died. And I don't know what that weird spell I did today in the classroom was. "Anyway," I shake my head to clear it. "This won't hurt anyone. I don't think it's bad if you use it as protection."

Stacia nods grimly. "I was hoping it would turn him into a toad. I was hoping he would lose the capacity to swallow. That he would drown in a mouthful of his own spit." I feel a chill. Yes. I know what she means.

The moon, waning and low, peeks out behind a dark cloud and looks down at us, impervious and uncaring. I think of Artemis, the moon goddess, who killed a man just for seeing her naked, and the thought makes me feel powerful, strong. Maybe I am a descendant of the goddesses, and my mother too. Women of magic, fierce birds. Deities of the sea and sky. I clear my throat.

"Drake MacLachan," I say, holding the jar to my chest, and I feel the magic rise up from the earth and move all around me. "I bind thee from causing harm." A sudden wind sweeps up from nowhere, and I have to raise my voice to be heard. "Drake MacLachan, I bind thee from causing harm." The third time, Stacia joins in. "Drake MacLachan, we bind thee from causing harm." Our voices are strong in the night, and the wind carries our voices and our intentions to the farthest reaches of the school.

The cherry tree is dropping blossoms and littering the dirt with pink flowers and I feel powerful. Stacia looks at me, her spiky dark hair whipping her eyes. She twists her body so that her back is against the wind and her hair blows out behind her. "Shit," she says, turning back to me, and suddenly the beam from a flashlight sweeps across the field.

"Someone's here," Stacia whispers. "Hurry."

We dig hastily, not doing the job we had wanted to do. I feel far less magical and powerful than I did moments ago. My breath is caught in my throat. What if we get in trouble? How would we explain ourselves? "Sorry, sir, we were casting a spell"? Once the hole is deep enough, we drop the peanut butter container in and quickly cover it with dirt. Stacia pats the mound with the back of her shovel.

"Hey!" a man's voice shouts. "Who's there?" The beam from his flashlight is on us, and he is walking quickly in our direction. We jump up and begin to run. We run, laughing, all the way to the park three blocks away, where all the stoners get stoned during lunch break.

The park at night is empty.

Stacia and I sit on the swings. The waning moon above us lights up the playground, and beside me, Stacia sighs.

"I'm sorry I wasn't able to stop him. I heard him talking to his friends; I knew last night was the night. But . . ." She drifts off, then shrugs.

"It's okay. I'm sorry no one tried to stop him for you," I say.

"I wouldn't have listened either," she admits. I feel heavy at the thought of her, carrying her secret alone. At least I've had her to talk to. She's had weeks with no one to confide in.

We rock back and forth on the swings, but slowly, not like little kids pretending to fly.

"Are you going to be okay?" Stacia's chin nearly touches her chest. She is looking down toward her own legs, but I wonder what she is really seeing.

I still see myself on the ground in the dirt. I still feel the pressure of his hand, the pain, like being split open. In that, I feel like something was released, something dangerous and angry. I don't know if I can control it. But I can't tell Stacia that.

"I'll be okay," I tell her.

CHAPTER TWELVE

Can't sleep. I close my eyes and all I can see is a cage against the night sky. Stars twinkle behind the bars of the cage like some false hope, bright and unattainable as the moon. Unattainable as a dead father. Or my past. Or my future. There's a pounding in my head, a slow rhythm like a death march. I reach my hand up behind my ear and twirl a finger around a small hunk of hair. And I yank. Until my closed eyes see only red. *Stupid girl*, the pounding in my head recites. *Pathetic. Prick tease. Little bitch. Waste of time.*

Finally I sleep. When I wake up, clumps of my hair lay scattered like chameleons on the floor.

❖

The next morning, Drake isn't in English, and by the time I get to class, a construction paper get-well card is being circulated. Olive shows it to the girl in the seat in front of me.

"Zoe, can you sign this for Drake? He was in a car accident last night."

"Oh my God." My hands fly to my face and a lump of guilt lodges itself in my throat. "Is he hurt?"

"He's not not-hurt," Olive says curtly, snatching the card from

Zoe and bringing it to my desk. "You should sign this, since you're, like, sleeping with him or whatever."

"Ew, I am not," I say, harsher than I meant, and as I push the card from my desk, it bends and crumples.

"Oh my God," Olive says, trying to flatten the card as she gapes at me. "You are such a bitch. He was nothing but nice to you, because he felt sorry for you. I can't believe what a bitch you are." All around me, people glare. I grab my bag and spend first period in the bathroom.

Leaning against the stall, I think of that weird picture I drew yesterday in class, the one with the spell. I thought it was silly. I thought it was laughable. But this is so not funny. I killed frogs. I put a boy in the hospital. Cheyenne was right about me. I am a monster. Drake split my body down the middle with his fingers and the old Lacy flew out. Demon girl. Fierce bird. There is no point in trying to be good anymore. No point in trying to be like Anna. It is my mother's blood that churns through my veins. Anna is soft and sweet, like a stuffed animal. My mother and I are all shit and edges and barbed wire. We are capable of pure evil. You don't want to get too close to us.

❖

At snack, Stacia grabs me and pulls me to a quiet corner. Her eyes are wide with fear. "We did it," she says. "We caused the accident with our spell."

"No," I say. "It was a binding spell. It couldn't hurt him. It's just to keep him from hurting others."

"What if it's keeping him from doing that by taking him out of the equation?"

I shake my head. "Magic doesn't work that way," I tell her. I can tell it doesn't help. I should tell her the truth, that I alone caused the accident. That with my own quiet spells, I turn everything to shit.

⁘

My mom gets out of bed from time to time, to make big pots of coffee or sit in the backyard, her long fingers trailing in the murky pool water. Her boss called a couple of nights ago, left an angry message on the phone. "Don't bother coming back, princess." My mother scowled and showed the phone her middle finger.

I leave her alone. I learned my lesson years ago, when she'd stop going to work and stay in bed, and I'd lie beside her, brushing her sweaty black hair with my fingertips. "I'm sorry you're sad," I'd say. But she would just roll away from me. I'd perform puppet plays using angels and monsters made from socks, and she'd tell me to get out, or pretend to snore. Once she threw a glass of water at me.

Who cares? I'm as tough as she is. A fierce bird, sharp beak, gilded wings. I don't need her to be my mommy.

⁘

It is Sunday, and I have invited my two friends, Stacia and Martin, to the house for breakfast. I may be a monster, but at least I have good friends. With that, there is something good in me still. My mom is lying in her bed watching cartoons, and every once in a while she bursts out laughing. Stacia and Martin sit as far from each other as possible, eyeing each other warily. But I'm not worried. They are both good people and they are both my friends. I know they will like each other.

I serve them cherry Pop-Tarts and kiwi strawberry Snapple, and we settle onto a blanket on the floor in the living room to eat. "I like your earrings," Martin finally says.

"Thanks," Stacia says, fingering the '80s-style miniature lightning bolts that hang down from her ears like chandeliers. "I like your orange socks," she says, referencing the ones he wears like gloves.

There now.

❖

On Monday morning, Olive and their friends aren't under the cherry tree. Maybe they can sense the intentions buried beneath the soil.

In the hallway, people look at me funny. I smile, but most everyone averts their eyes. One girl smiles at me a little, like she feels sorry for me. A group of girls see me coming, giggle, and turn to walk the other way. I close my eyes. The slut rumor is circulating, I guess. I head straight for English.

When I get there, Olive is already at her seat. "He has the number right there on his phone," she's saying. "It's not a rumor; it comes straight from her own mother." When she sees me, she stops talking and purses her lips like she's been caught at something and finds it funny. *Oops*, her expression says. *Busted, but oh well!*

My breath catches in my throat and I shiver. What is she saying about me? Is this about my mother? Martin comes in and his eyes find me, and he smiles at me the same sympathetic way as that girl in the hall. I want to go grab him and take him outside and find out what is going on, but I'm afraid of how it would look. That it would worsen whatever it is they're saying.

The bell rings and I try to breathe. Whatever it is they're saying, I have to make it through this period. I take a piece of paper from my bag and draw lavender stalks. Then lightning bolts like the ones from Stacia's earrings. Finally, Mrs. Kesey comes in, clutching a maroon-colored book in her hand, "Hey, guys," she says, hoisting herself atop her desk and holding the book against her baby bump. "Sorry I'm late. I thought I was out of the morning sickness phase, but I've been hugging the porcelain goddess all morning long. Anyway." She makes a flourishing motion with her hand. "This is *The Catcher in the Rye.* I read it when I was your age and it changed my life. When you read it, try not to think of it as a school assignment but your priest, therapist, and best friend, all rolled into one."

The next ten minutes are spent with us checking out our own maroon books. Then Mrs. Kesey returns our papers on archetypes, then a spelling quiz. The minutes tick by like the slow death march of tiny toy soldiers. Left . . . left . . . left . . . Olive checks her tattoo periodically. Yup, still there.

Finally the bell rings and everyone shuffles out. Mrs. Kesey also kind of pushes her way through the door. "Sorry, kids," she says. "Time to go revisit my breakfast." Megan Chan glances back at me, then whispers something to Olive and they crack up. Drake's friend Jacob leans in to hear what they are saying. I grab Martin and pull him out into the hallway.

"What is it?" I ask.

"It happens. Some women get nausea in the third trimester just because the baby's so big."

"Not that." I punch him, whispering fiercely. "What are they saying about me?"

"Oh, that. It's just a stupid rumor," he says, and I feel a pang. Martin doesn't have any friends aside from me, and even he knows what they're saying.

"What is it?" I ask again. I hold my necklace in my palm as it heats up.

Martin looks over my shoulder like he might try to make a run for it. Then he sighs. "They're saying Olive went to visit Drake in the hospital yesterday after school and she was playing with his phone and she saw your mom's name in his call log. So she was teasing him and he told her it wasn't you that called, it was your mom. But he wouldn't tell her anything, so she waited until he fell asleep, and then she listened to his messages. And there was one from your mom from a few nights ago. She said on the message that she knew you'd snuck out of the house to be with him, and she called him to tell him to be careful with you. I guess . . . what they're saying is . . . that your mom told him on his voice mail that you're crazy. Olive listened to it a bunch of times."

I exhale slowly. "Look, it's just a rumor," Martin says. "No one's going to believe it, not really —"

"It's fine." I hear how my voice sounds, sharp and mean, but I turn away from him anyway. Olive could have made the whole thing up. But why would she make it so detailed? My mom's name and phone number on his caller log. It could have been me, using the landline. But I never called Drake, not once.

⁜

By break, they are saying I am fresh out of an insane asylum — that's why I came to the school midsemester.

By lunch I was receiving shock therapy, and I bit the guy who was administering the shocks. Martin and Stacia sit beside me in the plaza. No one is under the cherry tree. "I guess the spell didn't work," Stacia says.

I bite my lip. "Maybe it did. Olive started the rumor, not Drake."

"What are you talking about?" Martin asks.

"Nothing," we both say quickly. Stacia must think I'm such a baby, messing around with spells and magic. Unless she believes the rumors and thinks I'm a raging lunatic.

All day long I feel eyes boring into the back of my head, people judging me, thinking their mean thoughts. I can't stand it, and I'm literally itching to get out. I scratch at my arms. I scratch at my burn mark. In the bathroom I pull out bits of my hair. In the old days I would have cut school, and I don't know what is keeping me here now. Some loyalty to that good girl I became, I guess. To that girl in Chico with her basket of herbs and sweet-smelling tinctures and pouches. But that girl has been replaced by a monster. And now everybody knows it.

I don't wait around after school to hear in what ways the rumor has evolved. Maybe I'm like the guy from *The Silence of the Lambs*, maybe I'm making a coat of human skin. I go to grab my bike, but the lock is stuck. Around me people wait for me to move so they can get to their own bikes. I can feel them watching me, waiting to see what I'm going to do, who I'm going to bite. Finally, I get it unstuck and I nearly tear it from the bike rack, desperate to get away.

❖

At home, I check Cheyenne's bed, but she's actually gotten out of it. She's not in the house, and she's not in the yard. I go into my room and play my father's guitar fast and furious. I strum at it hard. Maybe the strings will break.

My cell chirps, probably some jerk prank call, but the ID says Anna. I pick up without thinking. After asking me how I am ("Fine"), she launches right in.

"I want to come and visit," she says. "So do the Treehuggers. And Shell and Mechelle. We all want to take a road trip in the bus. Do you think Cheyenne would mind? We could meet you somewhere if she would."

I imagine them here. Anna. My best friends. But then they would see what I am. Monster. They would see who I am here. Crazy girl, mean girl, the girl I've tried so hard to stow away.

"I don't think so," I whisper. "I don't think it's a good idea."

"No?" Anna sounds confused. Simple Anna. She is cotton candy, not barbed wire and steel wool. "Well, we really miss you."

I say nothing nothing nothing.

"Is everything okay there?"

"Yes." No no no.

"Lacy, I'm coming there. Something's wrong. I can be there in an hour."

"No, look. I'm just having a bad day. I'm being a jerk and I'm sorry." I know I don't sound sorry, though.

"Oh. Well, that's okay. Everybody has bad days." Her optimistic tone makes me even more furious. I envision myself punching through walls. I envision my father knocking down the door. His rage my rage.

"I have to go," I say, practically choking into the phone. My vision is a channel on TV that doesn't come in. I put my head between my knees and try to breathe, but all I see are burning cows in a field. Maybe those kids are right, maybe I am crazy. It has been a long time since I've cut myself. But I have catalogued the drawers in the kitchen. I know which knives are the sharpest.

I take the paring knife and sit on the floor. I press the knife into my heel until blood pools. The fear and frustration releases along with my blood. Now I won't be able to take a single step without being reminded of what an awful person I am.

❖

I remember when my mom started messing everything up. Robbing houses, getting caught. It was the year I started kindergarten. I had just moved in with her full-time because the court had named her the primary custodial parent. After that she kept having to go back to court, the first time for arson, the next for petty theft. For a while she kept eluding the law. I remember the babysitters who watched me during her court dates. One of them told me if I ate all my peas, there would be a surprise for me at the bottom of my Princess Jasmine bowl. I ate all the peas, but there was no surprise, only the picture of Princess Jasmine with Raja, and I already knew they were there. We'd watch old reruns of *Little House on the Prairie*, and I'd imagine my mom before some crown-wearing puppet king like the ones on the TV shows I watched every morning. I imagined the way she'd appeal to the puppet king, the way he'd fall to his knees in mercy. And maybe he did. Until, suddenly, when I was eight, she went to prison for three months and I was sent for the first time to live with Anna and my dad.

I don't remember much of that time. I remember crying a lot. Missing her, longing for her until my entire body hurt. After she got out, we were allowed supervised visitation. We'd meet at McDonald's and she would just stare at me while I ate my hamburger, chewing slowly, trying to make our time together last. I hated that it had to end. I hated saying good-bye. I wanted to live with my mom, to bask in her glow, her beauty so piercing and dangerous. And eventually I got my wish. She got joint custody, and she took my dad to court for child support, and she won that too. But that was when she changed in other ways. She started taking pills that made her crazy and deranged; she'd lock me in the bathroom without food. Of course it wasn't the first time she'd done crazy mean things to me. There was the time when I was little that she tied me to a tree. The time she burned my wrist with a cigarette because I was asking too many questions. There was the time she lit our apartment complex on fire.

We moved again. All over Sacramento, off Stockton Boulevard, Florin, Oak Park. We must have moved six times the year I was twelve. I took to stealing. I started with Cheyenne's cigarettes, but then it was jewelry from my classmates and lip gloss and magnets from whatever stores we went into.

And then she disappeared. I came home from school one day and she was gone. That was when I started living off beans, salami, ketchup. Finally, I called my dad, who stayed the night and took me home to Chico the following morning. We kept waiting for her to come back for me, but she never did.

In the meantime, she kept the child support that was being garnished from my dad's wages. Every month, four hundred dollars came out of his pay and went into her bank account. I heard my dad tell Anna that he'd had a huge argument with the people at work who filled out the papers for his paycheck, and they said they couldn't stop without a court order. We couldn't get her to return it because we didn't know where she was. We couldn't take her to court for the same reason.

I would lie under my moon garden and look up at the glowing white flowers against the night sky. I thought of the sleep sachet I'd made for Anna, the one stuffed with hellebore and nightshade. I thought about the sugar I put in her perfume. It hurt my own feelings when I snubbed Anna now. I would say mean things to her and she would shrug them off, but I couldn't. I went inside. I saw how dark and mean it was in there. I didn't want that anymore. I didn't want to be the person who burned butterflies. I wanted to be the person who worshiped them.

It wasn't easy to change. I started by playing the role. I met friends at my school, Shell and Mechelle, and I complimented them on their clothes, but only when I meant it. I told them, "I'm so lucky to have you as my friends," and it didn't take long for me to believe it. And then it became the truest thing.

Finally, we just let her go. My dad figured it was worth her keeping the child support money, as long as she stayed far away from us. Anna found a detective who was willing to give us information whenever Cheyenne was caught doing something. Going to prison for extortion, for welfare fraud. Finally, my dad was able to get the garnishment stopped. A year after that, he died of prostate cancer. And with him, every last shred of good magic.

❖

To punish myself for cutting, I decide to take a walk. I put socks and tennis shoes on over my sores. Outside, I think of the old fairy tales Anna told me, the ones where people's feet ache and throb. The little girl in the Red Shoes, begging the executioner to cut off the shoes that won't stop dancing, and with them, her poor bleeding feet. The stepsisters in Cinderella — one loses a toe, the other a heel. And the Little Mermaid, who feels as though she is walking on needles and knives. A little cut on the heel is nothing. I should have sliced off my pale pink sole.

I don't set out to visit Myrna, but before long I realize that's where I'm headed. Myrna is out in front of her shop, picking spinach and chard from her garden.

"Hey," I say, walking in through the gate.

"Lacy!" Her eyes light up like someone special is coming, not a mean-spirited teenager with seeping sores.

"What are you doing?"

"Harvesting some greens for dinner." I think of our garden in Chico, the one I'd harvest from every night. I miss it, along with everything else. I miss the butterfly bush that drew all the butterflies. I miss the wild toad who ate our slugs at night and slept during the day in the toad house Anna made. "Come on inside, I'll make tea."

We sit in her weird kitchen at the monster alien table after Myrna brings me a steaming mug of chamomile. It's an iced tea day, the kind where you want to lie, catlike, in pools of sunlight on the porch, but Myrna always looks so cold, holding herself and shivering under her sweaters. I want her to drink giant sips, to make herself warm and strong.

"What brings you?" she asks.

"I'm having a bad day. I was mean to my stepmom. Cheyenne wouldn't understand. I know you're her friend, but . . ."

"No, that's okay. I do want you to feel safe here, Lacy. You can talk to me."

"Why are you so nice to me? Why do you want to be my friend?"

"Well, I like you," she says, as if she's never thought about it before. "I recognize something of me in you," she says after a moment. "We have something in common, I think." She takes the tea bag from her cup and wraps it around a spoon. I sip my own tea. It goes down warm and feels good. I guess I was cold too.

"I don't think we have much in common," I say. It sounds mean, and that isn't how I intend it. It's just that she seems like a nice person, and I'm not. But my foot is throbbing, and I don't even have the energy to explain.

"Well, then. Why are you having a bad day?"

"Some kids at school started a rumor about me. I guess it's not such a big deal, but —" I stop myself. I can't exactly tell her that my mom was the one who started it.

I try again. "I guess the reason I'm here is, I have a few questions about my mom. I know you'll say I should just ask her, but I've already tried that. She won't talk about it."

"Well, if it's between you and your mom, I probably shouldn't get involved." Typical adult response. "But there's no harm in asking. I'll answer what I can."

"She went somewhere for a while. It was like she just disappeared. One day she was still there, being a mom, talking about taking me to Paris, and the next she was gone. Do you know where she went?"

Myrna tilts her head to one side. "Hmmm," she says. "I don't know — your mom moves around a lot. Can you tell me more specifically when this was?"

When it was. It was three years ago, in April. There was a beat-up-looking house on our street, the front yard full of weeds and tall grass. But in the backyard the owners kept chickens and some bunnies. It was April, and a new litter of bunnies had just been born. The owners — an old couple — I don't remember their names — invited me into their backyard. Despite the way I looked, like a mean little kid who'd grown up too fast, they invited me back there to hold the baby bunnies. The kits — I remember that, the old couple called them kits — had huge feet, and their noses wiggled like funny vibrating triangles on a kids' TV show. When I moved in with my dad and Anna, I knew by the time I came back, those bunnies wouldn't be babies anymore. I wonder if they're still alive today. I don't know how long rabbits live.

"I remember," Myrna says, and for a moment I think she's remembering the bunnies too. "That was when she went down south to stay with her parents." I blink. I want to tell Myrna she has it wrong. Cheyenne doesn't have parents; she's been telling me that since I was tiny. She tells her own creation myth, in which she popped fully formed out of a dragon's head, a spin on the Greek myth of Athena. Even though I knew that wasn't true, I never imagined that I had grandparents. My father's parents died when I was a baby, and I just figured my mom's parents were dead too.

I drop my head on the glass table, carefully, so as not to break it. "I'm so confused," I say. My heel throbs. Myrna runs her fingers through my hair. Her fingers, like my own, are ice.

❖

At home, Cheyenne is sitting on the couch, petting a gray cat.

"Hey!" I say. "I thought you were allergic."

"I know! So did I. Well, they say the gray ones carry less allergens."

"Do you ever tell the truth?"

"Excuse me?"

"Why didn't you tell me I have grandparents? Why did you leave me alone in that house? I don't even understand why you took me from Anna. You don't love me." The minute it's said, I recognize the truth of it. I narrow my eyes. "You don't even know how to love."

Cheyenne's face darkens for a moment, but then it seems to clear. "Now relax," she says. "Let me make you some tea." She tosses the cat to the floor. I follow her to the kitchen.

"You told me you were allergic to cats. You told me that's why I couldn't bring Mr. Murm! I told you Mr. Murm was my best friend in the world, and you still said I couldn't bring him!"

"Shhh." She fills a mug with water and puts it in the microwave. "Please," she says. "You're hysterical. You need to calm down."

"Whose cat is that?" I don't know why I'm fixating on the cat. There is so much more to this than the cat.

"A man I met at the bar when I was still there. He has an orthodontic convention in Seattle and I told him I'd cat-sit."

"For how long?"

"Just until Monday. Next question?"

"You told me you don't have parents."

She sighs. "Oh, Lacy. They are bad people. I didn't want you around them." She hands me the cup of tea. I drink. It makes me tired.

"But you went to stay with them. Why didn't you tell me where you were? Why didn't you tell me where you were going? How could you just leave me here all alone?"

"You know, I'm the mom here. I don't owe you any explanations, but the simple truth is, I didn't know I was going. But someone was after me, someone bad. I had to get away for a while, and I knew that was the last place anyone would look."

"So someone was after you and you left me alone in the house? Doesn't that seem a little neglectful?"

"No one was going to hurt you. I knew that."

"How? How did you know that? Why didn't you take me with you?"

"I told you already! I didn't want you around my parents. I was trying to protect you."

I'm shaking with anger, but I yawn, and I struggle to get past it, the dull tiredness. "Okay," I say, trying to get my thoughts in order. I sit at the table. "I have one more question."

"Go ahead."

"Everyone at school is saying you called this guy, Drake. They're saying you told him I was crazy."

"Oh, I didn't say that," she says dismissively.

My eyes swim. I try to focus on her. Her tea always makes me feel so weird. Good, but weird. I wonder, not for the first time, what exactly is in it.

"But you did say something? You did call him?"

"Well, Lacy, what was I supposed to do? My only daughter was sneaking out at night. You thought I didn't know? I know everything you do. You're my blood; I can feel your thoughts coursing through my veins."

"Why do you say things like that? It's creepy."

"Don't you remember, darling? We are fierce birds. But the world belongs to us alone, you and me. I don't want you making the same mistakes I did, running off with the wrong boys. I just told that boy to be careful with you. I told him you had been through a lot, and you were fragile."

"But you didn't tell him I'm crazy?"

She sighs again. "I told him you were fragile. Delicate, something like that. I suppose I can see why he took it that way, but I don't think I said the word *crazy*."

"Mom! The kids at school are saying I just got out of a mental institution. They're saying I bit some guy. How could you do this?"

"Oh, Lacy, really. You think kids didn't tell rumors about me when I was your age? We frighten them. We are beautiful, we are interesting." She sits beside me and swings her full dark hair to the side. She moves like a goddess, tan and slender in her white dress. But cat hair clings to her belly and the area underneath. It is lewd, like a weird circus snapshot.

"I'm going to my room now," I tell her, too exhausted, unable to process it all. I think I should stop drinking my mom's tea.

⁂

I awaken in my bed, a little hungry and very cold. Evidently I fell asleep. Evidently I missed dinner. I go into the kitchen and make myself a turkey sandwich. I'm back to eating meat again. The gray cat is sleeping on the couch. I pick him up and try to take him to my room, but he hisses and scratches me and runs off.

From my bed, I start *The Catcher in the Rye*, homework for tomorrow. I don't get what all the buzz is about. The main character seems like a jerk. Kind of a sweet jerk, but still a jerk. But I like Mrs. Kesey, and I know she's passionate about the book, so I'll keep muddling through, just not tonight.

Instead, I go out into the cool evening to water my plants. Cheyenne is sitting cross-legged next to the swampy pool. She looks like she's meditating, and her hair floats like coils, like snakes, in the air. She really is beautiful. But she is so much more than her looks. Like a terrible child who seems peaceful when he sleeps, Cheyenne looks so gentle when she's at ease.

In case she is meditating, I walk quietly past her and turn on the hose. My plants are nearly dead. I can't understand it. Maybe it is the Sacramento soil. I never had this much trouble in Chico. That lone poppy plant flourishes, its blooms scarlet against its leaves. I pluck a leaf from it and smell it, and suddenly Cheyenne is behind me.

"What are you doing?" she demands.

"Nothing. I'm sorry. I was just —"

"You were just what?"

"I was just wondering why all my plants are dying. This one's so healthy. I don't know how to help my plants. Everything I touch dies."

As my eyes fill with tears, Cheyenne's fierce gaze softens.

"Now, that's not true," she says. "You know, I was thinking about that rumor. We could do something to get back at Drake for spreading it around." I shiver because part of me, the part that can't even for a moment forget being called those names and left crying against a tree, wants to. Wants to just keep casting spells until, like Stacia said, he loses the capacity to swallow. Until he's as broken as a bird that has flown into a window.

"I guess he was in a car accident," I say. "He's in the hospital."

"Oh my goodness, is he okay?"

I stare at her. It is so hard to know whether she's being sincere. "I guess so. I don't know. We aren't exactly friends anymore."

"Well, think about it." She reaches her hand out for the leaf I'd plucked. "If you want my help getting back at him, let me know. I don't know if you remember, you and I used to be pretty good at casting revenge spells on our enemies."

"I was five. I didn't have any enemies."

"So you do remember."

"Yes. I remember." I do, but I wish I didn't.

"Good. Our minds are powerful. Our minds can move mountains." She smiles. "In the meantime, you stick to your garden and let me tend to mine, all right?"

"Sure," I say, putting the leaf in her palm. She closes her hand around it and watches me as I go back into the house.

⁘

"Our minds our powerful," she had said. "Our minds can move mountains." Ancient wisdom, words I grew up hearing. It was those words that led me to do what I did on that night, so many months after Cheyenne's belly started to grow.

I lay in bed that night, imagining the thing inside her — an alien shrimp with a veiny skull and black eyes. If he were allowed to be born, then he would come between us, between me and my mother, between us and Paris. We had just started getting along and now this thing would come and take it all away. And I hated him. And I was jealous.

So I lay there imagining him, and in my mind he became still. His curled body unmoving. In my mind, he became dead. I whispered, *Dead, dead, dead.* I fell asleep with that image in my head. Beady black eyes clouded over with that death wisp of gray.

That night, there was blood everywhere. My mother moaning in the bath. Water was running and there was blood in the water and her face was twisted up in pain. Her moans shook the apartment. She took blood from her own body, where it flowed and flowed between her legs, and she took her bloody hand and rubbed it on the baby's head. She wrapped a silver chain around his ankle, and recited incantations as she held him to the mirror. As she did, I felt a jolt, like my own spirit was trying to fly away. I clenched my fists and held my ground, and before long, she tore the chain from the baby's ankle and threw it at the mirror. Then she stared into her reflection, biting her lip until it bled. I ran back to my room and hid beneath the covers until she came for me. "Get in the truck," she simply said. "We're going to the river."

"The baby?" I asked.

"A boy. But he's dead." I felt it then. Triumph in my heart. I was so bad I didn't even know to feel sorry.

CHAPTER THIRTEEN

Mrs. Kesey looks increasingly uncomfortable by the day. I know why she sits on the top of her desk — it's because her belly's too big to fit in the actual seat. She brings a big water bottle with her everywhere she goes, and she drinks from it constantly. It's mean to say she reminds me of a pig, especially since she's so nice. But with her pink skin and pregnant belly, I can't help but think it.

"God," she says, then, "mmmph."

"Are you okay, Mrs. Kesey?" Martin asks.

"This kid is playing hockey with my uterus," she says, which makes us all squirm, I'm sure. It makes me squirm, anyway. Who wants to think about uteruses?

Happily, she quickly launches into the subject du jour, *The Catcher in the Rye*. "What do you guys think?" she asks.

"It's funny," one of the football players says, "but kinda stupid."

"That Holden guy's sexy," Olive says. "You can tell he's really good-looking."

"But nobody talks like that," says one of Olive's friends. "Everyone's a phony and everything's ironical."

"And he says his friends are sexy, like, the guys," says a boy I don't know. "That's not cool, man."

"Well, the language might be antiquated, but the themes are universal." Mrs. Kesey shifts on her desk. "I want you to think about that as you continue reading. I want you to think about ways you can relate to Holden, ways where he might be having feelings similar to feelings you might have from time to time. Lacy? You don't look impressed. What do you think?"

"I don't really like it," I say. "I think he's kind of a jerk. He's so judgmental about everyone, but he doesn't seem that great either. He's a liar, and he keeps flunking out of schools, so he's not all perfect."

"Ah, good point." Mrs. Kesey goes to the dry-erase board. *Unreliable Narrator*, she writes. "Holden is what we call an unreliable narrator. We can often trust everything the narrator of a book tells us, but in this case, we can't. Like Lacy said, he tells us one thing, but we see him act in opposite ways. Can anyone think of any examples of this?"

Instead of examples, I think of myself, and suddenly I do relate to Holden Caulfield. If my life were a book, I'd be an unreliable narrator. I keep telling myself I want to be good, a good person, a good friend. But I'm not, and I've known it all along. I'm worse than a phony. Or maybe that's exactly what I am.

❖

We have a substitute for chemistry. While we file into class, she sits at Mrs. Burke's desk, reading a book. When the bell rings, she doesn't stand up. She doesn't even look up or take roll. We sit at our tables quietly for about a second before it dawns on us that this is going to be a free period.

Kids start to move around, switching seats. The noise level grows. The teacher buries her face deeper into her book.

"Let's go," I say to Martin, feeling suddenly daring and a little bit flustery.

We grab our books and head out to the hallway. Stacia has seventh-period history. We go to her room and catch her eye through the door window. She sees us and raises her hand, says something to the teacher, and is out.

The halls are empty. I used to cut class all the time when I was a kid, but for some reason I stopped. I guess it was part of my good girl campaign. We leave through the parking lot and cross the street and walk a couple of blocks to the park where Stacia and I went after the binding spell.

The park is quiet. At the playground, a few mommies push their kids on baby swings or wait to catch them at the bottom of the slide. The mommies watch us out of the corners of their eyes. We stop short of the playground and drop our bags in a sunny spot.

"Of all the classes to have to miss." I sigh, flopping down on the grass. "I wish that woman had been subbing my PE class instead."

"You and your science." Stacia grins. "Haven't you gotten the memo? Science is b-o-r-i-n-g?"

"No, it's not," I say, grabbing her and pulling her onto the grass beside me.

"So this is what people do when they cut class?" Martin sits beside us. "Talk about school?"

"No!" we say. For a minute I think about the old days, when I used to cut class. I would never have used that time to talk about school. I would use it to smoke cigarettes and shoplift from the bottle store down the street.

In Chico, my shoplifting capabilities grew. Instead of licorice ropes and potato chips, I'd steal CDs and incense, skull rings and rubber ducks with horns. I kept everything I took in a drawer in my bedroom. Even though I later donated everything to the Salvation Army, I still can't open that drawer without feeling guilty.

When I was a bad girl who stole and cut class, I would never have dreamed of spending my free time ditching class lying on the grass next to a playground with two friends, one a bit goofy, one a bit punk rock, and staring up at the clouds in the sky. But at the moment, it's exactly what I want to do. We lie there as the clouds form themselves into dragons, pirates, an avocado, a bird. We stay until the sky looks like its inches from our faces, and everything else has disappeared.

✣

That morning at the river, my mother dug a grave. The baby lay still and gray in a yellow blanket. The sky turned gold, then pink as the sun began to rise, and I watched my mother in the pale pink light as she worked, her face devoid of emotion. My own emotions battled like cartoon ninjas — Relief and its equally strong opponent Grief. No magic that morning. No God. Just my own ugly, victorious black soul.

✣

The security guard at Rite Aid makes me check my backpack. I almost turn away to go somewhere else because I hate that kind of thing, people who don't trust you just because you're a kid with a backpack. But who cares. Maybe I will steal something, just to show them I can do it.

But I don't. I hold a black eye pencil in my hand. It would be so easy. I could just slip it up my sleeve. But I don't want to.

I grab the cheapest box of black hair dye. The cheaper, the better. I don't need it to look good.

When I get to the cashier, I make a big deal about not being able to pay because my backpack has been confiscated. The cashier, a girl with purple eye shadow and a lip ring, smiles kind of rudely and hands me my bag. She's probably sick of the whole bag-check thing too.

At home, I take scissors from the kitchen into the bathroom and chop off my hair, letting it fall in clumps at my feet. The hair looks prettier, healthier, on the floor than it ever did on my head. I decide to leave it there on the ground. I'm not picking it up. I wet what's left of my hair in the sink and mix the dye.

I wish I had my bomber jacket, but I don't. I wish I could take my scissors to all my expensive black clothes and cut them to shreds, but I can't. Myrna made them. I touch the rose necklace. It is just too beautiful to consider damaging.

The dye stings where I pulled out my hair. My eyes fill with tears but I massage the color in. I imagine it seeping into my bloody scalp. Black dye pooling into my veins, turning my insides murky. Monster girl as monstrous on the inside as out. I wish I could scribble black all over my face, like I used to do to pretty girls in my picture books. Princesses with scraped-out eyes.

After rinsing out the hair dye, I run my fingers through my newly shortened, blackened hair and leave without giving a thought to where I'm going.

I could wait until late at night, and I could go to the hospital and visit Drake, cut my skin open and bleed onto his sleeping face so that he awakens to warm blood in his eyes. I could hitchhike downtown, hang out with the homeless kids and smoke their cigarettes. I wish I were wild and unpredictable, but I'm not. I go to Myrna's store, where everything looks sinister, but nothing is, not really.

Myrna greets me with a plate of cookies.

"I knew you were coming over today, I just knew it," she says, chipper as a little girl. "I'm a little bit psychic sometimes, and just an hour ago, I was like, I'll bet my friend Lacy is on her way. And here you are!" She doesn't mention my hair. I run my fingers through it again, just to make sure it's still short and weird. "I'll put tea on!" she says, and disappears into the kitchen.

Instead of following her, I walk around her shop. Demeter's Daughter, it's called. I know from homeschooling with Anna that Demeter is Persephone's mother. Persephone is the Queen of the Underworld. Her mother spends all winter mourning, while Persephone is ruling down below, and when Demeter mourns, crops die. But when Persephone returns each spring, Demeter rejoices, and everything turns lush and green.

So if the store is Demeter's Daughter, then it's Persephone's store. And if it's Persephone's, then maybe it's the underworld. Hades. Maybe that's why I like it here. Maybe that's why it makes me feel safe.

"Are you Persephone?" I ask Myrna, walking into the kitchen.

"Pardon?" Myrna is pouring tea.

"The name of your store. I wondered if you named it after yourself."

"Oh." She looks sad for a moment, and warms her hands with the teapot. "No, I'm not Persephone. I'm Demeter."

"You have a daughter?"

"No." She looks down at the table, so I leave it at that. "Sit down," she says. "Have some tea."

I take a sip, warm and sweet. It's regular tea, not like my mom's weird tea.

"You cut your hair," she says, just like that, with no judgment. She sounds sad.

"It's just hair," I say.

"I suppose." She sips her tea. "I probably shouldn't say this, but it doesn't suit you. You look like you're trying too hard to be someone you're not."

"I don't know who I am."

"Well. You're a teenager, that's normal."

I think about Holden Caulfield, calling everyone a phony. Is Holden a phony? Am I? Maybe Holden isn't as judgmental as he seems. Maybe he's just trying to figure out who he is.

"Whenever I'm around my mom, I start acting like her. I can't control it." I shouldn't be telling her this, but I'm here. I don't know why I've come. But I can't talk to Anna and I sure can't talk to Cheyenne.

"And you don't want to act like your mom?"

"I didn't use to. But then something bad happened to me, and I didn't mind acting like her for a while. But now I'm being mean to Anna again, and she's never been anything but great to me. I miss her so much, but I don't even think she'd like me if she could see me right now. I've become bad again."

Myrna reaches across the table and takes my hand. "Oh, Lacy, you're not bad."

"But I am. I know you have to say I'm not, and I know probably you can't even see it, but I am."

"Hmm." Using her left hand, Myrna takes a drink of her tea. "Maybe you want to be bad, just a little bit."

"Why would I want to?"

"Well, think about it. If you're just bad, then you can do anything you want. You can be cruel to people, you can hurt even yourself. And when you're asked to account for it, you can just shrug your shoulders and go, 'Oh well, I'm bad.' It seems a little liberating, doesn't it?"

I shrug my shoulders. I suppose it does.

"But I really am. I cast a revenge spell on a boy, and the next day he got in a car accident. He's been in the hospital."

Myrna nods slowly. "That's bad. That was a bad choice. But we all make bad choices. God knows I have. So now it sounds like you have another decision to make. You can continue to make bad choices, or you can learn from that and move on. You can prevent yourself from making the same bad choices in the future. But only you can control that. Not me, not your mom, not anyone." She takes a spoonful of sugar from a glitter skull bowl and stirs it into her tea. "You know, I do believe your mom is just a little bit sick. That's why she has a hard time with some rules, that's why she keeps ending up in prison." Suddenly my body freezes up. Myrna is supposed to be my mom's friend, her protector. If she can betray my mom, then she can betray me. I told her too much. I shouldn't even be here.

"I have to go," I say, pushing my tea mug across the table.

"Are you sure? Lacy, I hope I didn't say the wrong thing."

"No, you didn't. I just have to go now. Thanks for the tea." I leave before she can walk me out. On the way, I pocket the glitter skull sugar bowl from the table.

❖

The knives in the silverware drawer sing to me as I walk through the kitchen. I pause, press the back of my wrist to the drawer. It feels good when I cut myself. I like the way the blood looks, the way everything feels so sharp and clean. But I hate how stupid I feel afterward. How lost and stupid and alone. I press my wrist hard against the drawer, but I don't open it. I hit the drawer with my wrist, and then I go to my room.

I feel bad about taking the sugar bowl. I shouldn't have done it. Myrna was probably just trying to be nice. I place it on the windowsill. It glints in the afternoon sun. Then I dig through my bag for my cell and call Anna. She doesn't answer.

CHAPTER FOURTEEN

I have captured the gray cat. I don't know when his owner is coming back for him, but he's late. I don't care. I will make this cat like me. I will make him love me. Even though, at the moment, he is pressed against my makeshift nature table, hissing at me.

My phone chirps. Anna.

"Lacy?" she says after I answer. "I'm sorry I missed your call. How are you?"

"I'm doing okay," I tell her. "I mean, you know." I shrug, even though she can't see me.

"Mr. Murm misses you. He's with me right now. Do you want to say hi?"

I sniff and say, "Hi, Mr. Murm," and I laugh when I hear him murm in reply. He doesn't actually say "murm" anymore. He says "meow" like a regular cat. "I miss him too," I say. "I miss you too."

"Any chance of you coming up for a visit?"

"I don't know. I'll ask Cheyenne. But I wouldn't hold my breath."

"Just tell me what you want, Lacy, and I'll make it happen. I don't know what to do for you right now."

I nod into the phone. I know what she means. It's not the type of thing she can understand. She's not my real mom, after all.

I push the END CALL button without saying good-bye. When it starts chirping again, I leave the room. I hate the sound of chirping now. It's grating and babyish. It's the sound a little girl might choose, a girl who believes in fairies and magic. A monster would never choose a ringtone like that. I'll have to find something more suitable.

✢

The orthodontist returns in time for dinner. I think he is here to pick up his cat, but he settles in, he stays too long. At dinner, he reaches for more of the mashed potatoes Cheyenne made by adding water and butter to a packet.

"Lacy," he says. "Has anyone ever told you you need braces?" I close my mouth and shake my head. I don't need braces. I have perfect teeth — my dentist in Chico said so. This is my mom's work. She wants to lock me in a steel cage. First my teeth, then she'll make for me a corset of bones. And rose-colored thorn shoes for my feet.

I leave the dinner table early. As I walk into my room, I hear Cheyenne say, "She is so much like her father."

And something lights up inside me. A little glimmer of hope. I'd forgotten about that. I'm not either Cheyenne or Anna. It doesn't have to be one or the other. I have my father inside me too. The man who took me on moonlit canoe trips down the river. Who took me to the observatory to see the stars and to the Blue Room Theatre to watch midnight plays. Who dressed in a chicken suit in support of his Treehugger friends. And that's when I know. My father wasn't abusive. He may have been angry sometimes,

142

but everyone gets angry sometimes. Anger is an emotion, and emotions are good. I'll ask Anna about it, but I already think I know what she'll say. That none of it's true. Because birds don't come to the funerals of abusive husbands and fathers.

✛

After he died, Anna and I wandered through the house like ghosts. Mr. Murm went back and forth between us both, like a little nurse, licking our tears and kneading our empty bellies with his black paws. I slept in Anna's room. Part of me was afraid she wouldn't want me, that I'd end up in an orphanage somewhere, eating gruel from a rusty metal bowl. But I think deep down I knew she wouldn't let me go, not without a fight. We lay in her bed, studying one of my dad's old books about the stars. Searching for answers. Like characters from one of our fairy tales. Stepmother. Black cat. Little match girl.

✛

My hands are cold. My feet are icy. It is May, a hot month in Sacramento, yet I dress in sweaters and I am still cold.

At school, I huddle at my desk and try to keep from shivering. Olive watches me out of the corner of her eye. Her eyes are always on me. She whispers things to her friends as they pass me and they laugh. It isn't enough that she has started a rumor. She wants to take me down.

They don't hang out under the cherry tree anymore. They haunt the halls, their mean eyes peering out beneath glittery eye shadow. "Loser," they call me. "Witch," they call me. They make me nervous, the way they watch me, with their glittery eyes and blank zombie faces. I don't know how much they know.

"Poor little psycho bitch," Olive says as they all walk past my locker. "I hear her mom's been trying to find a spot for her in one of the local loony bins, but none of them want her."

I could cast a spell against her. I could inflict sores on her legs and excruciating pain to her stomach. But I won't.

Stacia bares her teeth at her, growling. Sweet Stacia, who would never hurt anyone, not even a fly. Except maybe Drake, if she had a chance.

"You're so awesome," I tell her. She glares at me. It's okay. She knows she's awesome, and she knows that I know.

⁝⁝

After school, I find Drake's address on the Internet and ride my bike to his house. His mother answers the door. She is chic and tiny with short black hair and hazel eyes, Drake's eyes. I tell her I'm a friend from school, and she points me to his room.

He's lying in bed and medicine bottles crowd his nightstand. His room is dark and gross. The walls are stained yellow and there is dust and clutter everywhere. When he sees me, he groans.

"Oh God, Fin. What do you want?"

I step over clothes and CDs to get closer to his bed. "There's something I need to tell you," I say.

"What? I'm a dick. Whatever."

"That's not it."

He stares at me. His eyes look heavy and drugged. "So?"

"Look, it's going to sound stupid, but it's my fault you were in that accident. I cast a spell on you the day before in English class." It sounds so stupid when I say it, and I'm not surprised when he laughs.

"Jesus, Fin, how old are you? You cast a spell? Like a witch in a bad TV show? Your mom was right about you. You are crazy."

My eyes fill and he seems to notice. Uncharacteristically, he looks sorry for a minute. "You didn't cause the accident. I was driving too fast. I was pissed off at my dad and I was driving too fast and part of me even wanted to wreck my dad's car. He's an asshole." His face hardens and he swallows. "But whatever. Blame yourself if you want. Whatever makes you happy."

For a moment, I'd almost felt a connection with Drake. But the moment is gone. I nod and leave his room, shutting the door behind me.

❖

The orthodontist, who likes to be called Dr. Ryan (even though his first name, not his last name, is Ryan), wants to know how school was. I'm not kidding. I walk through the door, and the very first thing he says to me is, "Hey, kiddo! How was school?" Like he's my father and we're in some cheesy sitcom from the 1950s. *Just swell, Daddy-O!*

"It was fine," I mumble, going into the kitchen for some mint and ginger iced tea.

"Lacy," my mother calls after me. "Dr. Ryan wants to take us out to dinner. Isn't that nice?"

"My treat!" Dr. Ryan says. I have entered the twilight zone.

"Great," I mumble. I go into my room and close the door behind me.

Moments later, I can hear them arguing.

"Don't tell me how to raise my daughter," my mom says. He says something, and she says, "I am her goddamn male role model."

Dinner never happens. Voices rise and fall. They talk and argue into the night. After my homework is all done, and I have catalogued my herbs, I go into the kitchen, where I find a frozen pizza. I heat it up and eat it in my room. When I go to sleep, they are still in her room talking. Voices loud, voices quiet, him loud, her loud, him quiet, her loud. I am not awake when he leaves. But by the time I'm ready to leave for school the next morning, she is alone in her bed. She calls out to me as I pass her room.

"Dr. Ryan's gone," she tells me.

"I noticed."

"I mean he's history."

"Are you okay?"

"I think I'll live." She sighs. "He was rich, though."

"Yeah."

"And really cute."

"Okay."

She snorts. "He wanted you to call him Dr. Ryan."

"I know, he was lame."

"Yeah," but she leans back on her bed, kind of nostalgic-looking.

"Mom, I was wondering. Memorial Day weekend is coming up. I was hoping I could go visit my friends in Chico."

"And stay with Anna?"

"Yeah, I guess. If that's okay."

She pushes her hair back with her fingertips and yawns. "I suppose," she says. "Whatever."

"Thanks," I say. I bend down to kiss her cheek. The gesture surprises us both. "Later, Mom," I say.

"Dr. Mom to you," she calls after me.

❖

Gym is still my least favorite period of the day. Now we are practicing the divine art of modern dance. Fantastic. Olive and her clique watch me try to practice my final dance. They sit on the bleachers and laugh behind their hands as I circle my arms wildly to the music. My dance partner, Simone, keeps yelling at me to "tighten it up." But when I try to tighten it up, I move like a robot, in small jerky bursts. Simone has had it with me. She watches me too, frowning and shaking her head.

After gym class, I go to my locker for my clothes, but they aren't there. Olive is laughing with her friends, wearing only a white bra and gym shorts. I walk up to her.

"Have you seen my clothes?" I ask.

She glares at me. "Um. You're wearing them." Her friends snicker.

"Not my gym clothes. My real clothes."

"Your real clothes, hmmm. Maybe I have seen them. Oh no, you only wear black. The clothes I saw were gray."

What does that mean? The clothes she saw were gray. I look in the shower, I look in the sink. There. My silk wrap top and loungy pants are crumpled in the sink, turning lighter and lighter. Someone has poured bleach all over them. I walk back to Olive and whisper menacingly in her ear.

"Listen to me," I say, my cold voice a surprise, my boldness even a shock, but I continue. "You don't know what I'm capable of. But I will make you pay in ways you never even imagined were possible. Just wait." I move my head slightly away so I can read her expression. Her eyes are wide open, her mouth is parted. She is terrified. I have her. "You won't even know when it's coming. But it will come, again and again. I never rest."

When I step away, Olive is trying to compose herself, but she's scared. I'm a little scared too.

I might be just a little bit like my father, but my mother is still in my bones. She is swimming through my blood.

❖

I'm in a bad mood until chemistry, my solace class, my comfort zone. The minute I walk into the room, the darkness drains from me, the cool of my blood. Chem is hard for me, harder than biology, but it wakes up a part of my brain that I didn't know was in there, and I love it. I love how everything makes sense, and I like figuring out how all the numbers fit. This week, we have been studying the colors of chemicals, and today is lab day. We're doing the flame test lab, which means we get to burn things, and that is exciting for Martin and me both. Mrs. Burke passes out the Bunsen burners and wire loops, and Martin and I immediately start fighting about who gets to do the burning.

"You have neater handwriting," he tries, passing me the comp book.

"You don't want to burn your orange sock-gloves," I counter.

"We'll take turns," he says, and I nod, taking the book from him.

We switch off burning metals and writing the color of the flame next to the element into our comp book. Sodium is orange, and copper is blue green. Potassium is pink like petals from a cherry tree in spring. The writing in our comp book is so neat and clean. I watch as the electrons move from the ground state to an excited state and give off energy in the form of color.

Maybe I'll be a chemist when I grow up. An herbal chemist, if there is such a thing. There are a lot of concepts I haven't totally gotten my head around, but I love how everything fits together so neatly. Positive and negative, metal and nonmetal, protons and neutrons. I love the periodic table, how there's an order to everything.

It's so beautiful in the way it's structured. Everything has a number and a place and it all adds up like a map to the universe.

I think of ancient alchemists turning elements to gold. Base metals to noble metals. I would like to do that. I see myself in the future, gathering my herbs and extracting their components. I'll have a periodic table on my bedroom wall, and I'll consult it for answers, looking for links between humanity and the cosmos. Looking for the answers of the universe.

❖

In my room, I gather my sweetest-smelling herbs and tinctures. Vanilla beans in a jar. Rose petals and wild strawberry. I am going home, even if only for a weekend. And even though I can't be as nice as Anna, I can be more the girl I once was. "She is so much like her father," my mother had said. And I am. My mother is darkness and venom. It scares me when I act like her. Anna is cobwebs and song. She makes me sane. But me, I am like my father.

In Chico, gardens thrive and swans sing serenades to turtles. Egrets, not fear and sadness, have been known to follow me home from school. And I will be going in only a couple of days. The hills will turn from green to gold. I can't want this too much. If you want something too much, it won't happen. But I want this. I want this too much.

CHAPTER FIFTEEN

At school, I try not to imagine that she will still be in bed when I get home, that she will refuse to take me to Chico for the long weekend as promised. Even if she does, I can just call Anna to pick me up. I call her at break to put her on alert.

"She just broke up with someone," I tell her. "If she's feeling depressed, she might not be getting out of bed."

"No problem," Anna tells me. "I'll be ready with the bus. Just call me after school if you need me."

At lunch, I sit with Stacia and Martin beneath the cherry tree. Olive has left me alone all day, and her friends have been ignoring me too. I won't really do anything to get back at her. Although I could.

"Guess what," Stacia says, her dark eyes twinkling. "Olive has started a new rumor."

"Great," I groan.

"No, I think you'll like this one. She said Drake's back at his house, and she's been trying to nurse him back to health. I guess she thinks her duties are above and beyond." She snickers. "In any case, he tried to seduce her. But then she said he couldn't get it up."

I widen my eyes, nodding. I wonder what would have happened if we hadn't cast the spell. Would he have tried to hurt Olive too? I shake my head. It doesn't matter; it's none of my business anymore.

I propose a toast to us, and we clink drinks, me with my pomegranate juice in a bottle, Stacia with her Diet Coke, and Martin with his Gojilania goji and mangosteen juice (foods with funny names diet).

I have friends and nice clothes and a warm bed at night. I feel a surge of well-being course through me. Every once in a while, that happens. I'll just be sitting there, minding my own business, when all of a sudden I feel good, like everything is right in the world, and I am alive and it is amazing.

But like I said, I wanted it too bad. When I get home from school, Cheyenne is sitting on a chair at the kitchen table. A red candle burns, illuminating the dark sheen of her hair.

"Hello," I call, but she doesn't turn to me. Her hair streams down the side of her face, and I can't read her expression, but something is wrong.

"Mom?" I go to her in a panic. "What is it? Are you okay?" Her head slips off her hand and bangs the edge of the table. Her eyes are rolled back into her head, and her tongue hangs limply from her mouth. "Mom!"

Her head on the table, she nods weakly. "Wha. Lashy," she slurs.

"Mom. Stay there." I grab my phone, dial 911. The woman stays on the line with me until I see the red flashes though the window.

Then there are two men in the house. They move her onto the couch.

"What did she take?" one of them asks me.

"I don't know. I got home and she was like this."

He lifts a bottle I hadn't seen off the floor. The other one puts a tube down her throat. Cheyenne is gagging and coughing and crying. Her eyes are wild. How could she do this? What did she take? I can feel the thick tube in my own throat, choking me, and my own eyes fill with tears. The red flashes light up the walls, blood on blood, my mother crying gagging sobbing on the couch.

⁂

The hospital room is quiet and white. There is a gash on Cheyenne's forehead from where she hit it on the table. She lies back, an IV in her arm. "I'm sorry," she whispers to me.

"What did you take?"

"A lot of Xanax. A little vodka. Honey, please don't cry, I can't stand it."

"Were you trying to kill yourself?" I ask.

She wipes at my tears with her long, pale fingers and leans up to kiss me on the head. I feel it then, that current that runs between us, that current that means we belong to each other. Then she pats the hospital bed beside where I'm sitting, and I lie next to her, the tears still coming, and my mother brushes the hair from my face. After I settle down, we lie on our backs and she holds my hand. She doesn't say anything about the cold of my skin.

⁂

I close my eyes and the memory returns. The binding spell I did on my mother. I put the spell in an empty wine bottle and buried it below the crumbling front porch of the old hotel we lived in for a couple of weeks. But later, she held the bottle in her hand. She unwrapped the twine with her long red fingernails. Her red lips moved in anger, and I lay curled in a corner of a couch on the front porch, so scared.

I shoot straight up in the hospital bed, my mind messy with thoughts. If the binding spell had worked, then she wouldn't have been able to hurt herself with vodka and pills. And if the binding spell hadn't worked, then she might have been responsible for my father's death after all.

I shake her. "Did you kill him?" I ask. I sob as I shake her.

"What the fuck?" she says, her eyes fluttering open.

I take a breath and try to figure out what I'm asking. "Did you cause my dad's cancer with magic?"

"No, of course not." Her eyes are wide and innocent, and I don't believe her. She reaches for me. "You know I wouldn't. You know I promised." Promised what? I don't get what she's saying. "Look, calm down for a minute here, Lacy. Why are you asking me this? Why now?"

"I thought I did a binding spell. So that you couldn't hurt Dad and Anna."

"You did."

"Okay, but I just remembered that you found it. And you removed the bind."

"Well, yeah, Lacy, you buried it beneath about a centimeter of dirt. It was the easiest thing in the world to find. And when I found it, I shouted at you, and you cried for a few minutes and then you shouted back. You were pretty scary, actually. And I realized how worried you were, how much they mattered to you, and I'm still your mother, whatever you think. Don't you remember this?"

I shake my head no.

"I promised you on that day that I wouldn't use magic on your dad or Anna. And I've kept my promise. Whether you want to believe it or not, that's your choice."

I nod, slowly. Maybe I do remember, a little. And maybe I shouldn't, but I believe it. "I believe it," I say, and my necklace again warms my chest.

❖

Memorial Day weekend is spent in the hospital. Anna is not happy with me, or maybe she's just mad at Cheyenne, but she sounds angry when she talks to me. She thinks Cheyenne is just manipulating me. But she doesn't understand. I'm trying to do the right thing, and the right thing is to stay with this woman, my mother. I know it's what Anna would do. And my father. It's what he would do too.

Cheyenne is my mother. I don't always like her and I don't even think I always love her, but she is mine.

Together we lie in her hospital bed, playing cards or watching the TV. The nurses bring me vouchers for the cafeteria and I spend them on pizza, soda, and fries. My mom is brought trays full of Jell-O and lemon freeze and milk, and she eats all her food like a good girl. I offer her my pizza, but she shakes her head. Sometimes, at night, I wake up to find her holding me. I don't remember her ever touching me this way before. I begin to let myself love her again.

Myrna drove me back home so I could pick up some of our things, and when I came back, I brought with me a tincture made from plantain and apple cider vinegar for the gash on her forehead. Uncomplaining, she lets me apply it with a cotton ball. The tincture will pull out the pain and help her heal.

On TV, a commercial for mattresses comes on. This new mattress, the spokesman declares, will dramatically reduce your time spent tossing and turning.

"I like tossing and turning," I say. "It keeps my arm from falling asleep."

"It's the only way I get any exercise," my mom says, and we laugh. We laugh with each other. "I'm sorry about your weekend with Anna," she says.

"It's okay," I tell her. "Anyway, Anna is going to drive down next Saturday if that's okay. And she's bringing Mr. Murm. Since you're not allergic to cats anymore, do you think Mr. Murm can stay?"

My mom smiles at me and touches my wrist, just above the spot where she once burned it. "I don't see why not," she says.

❖

Finally, my mom is discharged. We go home and she climbs straight into her bed. I bring a chair from the kitchen and sit beside her. She isn't going to make me go to school. We play Scrabble and hangman, and I go out for movie rentals. Every morning, I get coffee and croissants, which we eat from white paper bags. We keep candles lit and avoid mirrors. Neither of us has showered in days.

❖

By Friday evening, I decide it is time for us to get out of bed. I ransack the refrigerator and find chard, onions, garlic, and carrots, all of which I bought over a week ago. Fortunately, none of it seems to have gone bad. Fortunately, Anna taught me how to cook — not a lot, but a little. I can make twice-baked potatoes and guacamole and rice cooked in vegetable broth with onions. I can make pasta and pizza crust. And soup. I can make soup.

I sauté the onions and garlic in butter and start a large can of chicken broth to boil in a pot. I want everything to be nice. The next-door neighbors have a garden of wildflowers, yellow ones with green caps like gnomes, and purple ones like little bells. I go outside to pick some, hoping no one sees. I know not to pick flowers from other people's gardens, but they have so many, and I really want the table to look pretty. I want Cheyenne to like me right now. Anna is coming tomorrow, and I want Cheyenne to be on her best behavior.

When the soup is ready, I pour it steaming into two bowls. I would season it with herbes de Provence if we had any, but all we have is salt and pepper. I can't use herbs from my garden; they're all dead.

"Mom," I call, and in a minute she comes shuffling out of the bedroom without me having to call her a million times. She wears her kimono and shiny blue slippers with gold embroidery. Slippers for a queen.

"Smells good," she says, going to the cupboard and pulling out a bottle of her expensive white wine with the cherry blossoms on the label. She also pulls out two glasses. "Will you join me in a glass?"

"Sure," I say, although I don't know if I'll be able to stomach it. White wine in a Dixie cup, metal in my mouth. She pours the wine into the glasses.

"Cheers," Cheyenne says, and we drink. It doesn't taste like Drake's wine. It tastes like a fairy wood, oak trees and pine trees, gnomes in their little mushroom houses. Drake's wine tasted like feet.

The soup is delicious if I do say so myself. It is hot and salty. We haven't eaten anything hot in days. We've been living off croissants and yogurt and CHEETOS. My mom reaches over to refill my glass. I didn't realize I'd emptied it.

"We should get drunk together," she says. "Wouldn't that be fun?"

I laugh, surprised. "Are you serious? Okay, why not?" I say. Shrugging away the questions in my mind: Why does she want me to get drunk tonight? So I'll be hungover tomorrow and not have fun with Anna? I shake my head and try to relax. I'm just glad that she's out of bed. I'm just glad that she isn't being mean.

After dinner we sit on the love seat in in the backyard, the open bottle of wine on the porch between us.

"Did I ever tell you about the time I went to San Miguel de Allende?"

"No," I lie. It's my favorite story. She's happy when she tells it. Maybe it was the happiest time of her life.

"I didn't? It's where I got those shoes. You know, the brown and red stripy ones with the heels."

"Oh yeah," I say, and I settle in against the pillows to listen.

"Your father and I went there when I was pregnant with you. We stayed in this great little hotel at the top of a hill. You could see the rooftops of people's houses. Their laundry hanging on the lines. There were so many colors there. I never saw color like that, before or again.

"We went to El Jardín, and I was captivated by the church. *La parroquia*, it was called, and it cast a glow during the day, but at night it was lit from within and the whole thing was gold. There was a magnificent white crucifix on the top, and the first time I saw it, in the late afternoon, I thought it was a silver angel lit by the sun."

"Sounds pretty." I help myself to more wine.

"It was incredible. Anyway, we were there in El Jardín one afternoon. Some mariachis were playing their instruments, and there was a woman selling jewelry. Your father and I looked at what she had, and when my eyes fell on this silver ring, you kicked me from inside. It was the first time I felt you kick. The ring was amethyst, set inside a silver spiral. I loved it. Your father bought it for me; he didn't even try to bargain down." This is my favorite part of the story.

"That night in our hotel room, I swallowed the ring. I wanted you to have it. I knew you liked it."

"I did," I say. "Thank you."

"I told your father I lost it, so he bought me those shoes instead. I was so happy then." She sighs.

"It sounds like it was really nice." I pat her back.

"I wish I could go back in time." I nod. I know what she means. What if we could go back in time? Back to a time when she loved my father and my father loved her. What if we could alter everything, just push the RESET button like you can do on a clock? Would I do it? I might. I think I would.

"If I could go back in time, I'd change what I did to your baby." My eyes fill with tears, and I pour the last of the woodsy wine into my glass. Cheyenne leans away and studies me.

"What you did . . ." She doesn't look mean, or mad. Just surprised.

"Yes, what I did. You know it was me. You'd told me our minds were powerful. You'd told me that they could move mountains.

So that night when he died, I'd been lying in bed, imagining him dead. I saw it in my mind, and I wanted it so much that I made it come true." I study her expression. Her eyes are wide. "I thought you knew that."

"Lacy," my mom laughs, a surprised laugh, free of bitterness. "You can't kill a baby by not wanting it. If you could, everyone would be an only child."

"But how do you know? I thought it, and I wanted it, and then he died."

"If anything, you saw what was already true. Lacy, the baby was already dead. I would have told you before if I knew you blamed yourself. He'd been lost to us for days. I went to the doctor earlier that week, and they hadn't been able to find a heartbeat. They offered me a D&C, which is a kind of surgery, or said I could just wait and miscarry on my own. I decided to wait, have him at home." She looks at me for a minute, then tries to pour herself a fresh glass of wine, but I've drained the bottle. She takes my glass from me, takes a sip.

"You aren't going to feel good tomorrow," she says.

"It's okay," I say. A feeling washes over me. For years I've carried this inside. But it wasn't my fault. The baby was already dead. It changes everything. It means that I'm not such a monster. That maybe I'm no monster at all.

I still cast a horrible spell on Drake. Maybe it caused the accident, and maybe it too was only a coincidence.

I lean my head back on the love seat. Everything is soft edges. The tip of the roof meets the night sky, and the waning moon is a sliver. My eyes begin to drop, and everything spins a little above me. But it isn't bad. I listen to the sound of Cheyenne humming a

159

little, her sweet voice. Sometimes I can't remember what it is about her I don't like.

⁜

When I wake up, my head hurts and my mouth is a little cottony. I take my tincture of willow bark to the kitchen and drop some in a cup of cold water, and I drink it, knowing it will help my headache. Then I make myself a cup of nettle tea to sip. My eyes want to shut, but I'm not going to let a little hangover get in the way of my day. I've been wrong all this time; I'm not a monster, and Anna is coming this morning with Mr. Murm. I wash my hair, brush my teeth, and put on some of my old clothes.

"Don't you look sparkly clean," Cheyenne says when I come to her room to say good-bye. I guess the spell of us getting along has broken. "Anna's little good girl. Her little Pollyanna."

"Please don't," I say, and surprisingly, she stops. She holds her hand out and turns her head. "Have fun," she says.

"Will you be okay?"

"I'm sure I can take care of myself for a couple of hours."

"You aren't going to —"

"Lacy, we've been over this. I wasn't trying to kill myself. I just needed to calm down a bit."

I look at her. Maybe I shouldn't leave. But I can't babysit her for the rest of my life. "Be good," I tell her.

"Yes, Miss Polly," she says.

⁜

Anna arrives at ten sharp, the low grumbling sound of our Volkswagen bus announcing her arrival before she's in sight. I unexpectedly tear up at the noise. In another lifetime, it was the sound of my dad arriving home from work.

160

In case my mom is watching through the window (and she is, of course), I do not bound over to the bus like an excited puppy. I slowly rise from the chair on the porch and walk down the steps. But Anna is not thinking. She jumps from the bus, runs up, and hugs me. "Lacy, oh my gosh, you're taller, why did you do that to your hair — I can't believe it's only been a month; you look so grown-up!"

I have to disentangle myself from her arms. "You brought Mr. Murm?" I ask.

"Yes!" Anna says cheerfully, but her face falls. I have already disappointed her. She had expected happy-go-lucky Lacy, not the fierce bird I have once again become. But I remember what I learned last night. The knowledge glows within me. Anyway, I don't want to be a fierce bird today. At least I'm not wearing any eyeliner. "He's in his carrier. Let's drive somewhere, and then we can let him out."

I direct her to McKinley Park. In the meantime, I hold Mr. Murm's carrier on my lap and whisper at him through the holes. "Hello, Mr. Mr.," I say. "I have missed you so." But Mr. Murm, instead of murming or meowing and nuzzling his black body close to the side of the cage, hisses and retreats to the far corner. From there he regards me with wide frightened eyes. It must be because he's not used to the carrier. We usually only use it to take him to the vet.

But when we get to the park and let him out of the carrier, he darts into some unknown corner of the bus. It's a '71, older than Anna herself, and it's full of strange dark nooks. "Mr. Murm," I call softly, but he won't come out.

"I don't understand," Anna says. "He was fine for the drive. Something must have spooked him." I know what we are both

thinking. Something spooked him all right. It was me. I'm not
out of this yet.

✣

After feeding ducks at the park for a while, we decide to pick up
sandwiches at the natural foods co-op, and then we drive back
to the river. It's another hot day, and Anna fans herself with
her hand. "Here," I say jokingly, putting my hand to Anna's
forehead.

"Lacy! Your hands are freezing!"

"I know. They've been that way since I got here."

"Oh." Anna looks at me strangely. "Have you been smoking
again?"

"No." I sound ruder than I mean to. "Why?"

"I don't know, I've heard it's bad for your circulation. It might
explain why your hands are cold."

"Well, I'm not smoking," I say, and I resent having to say it. I
feel like she should know me well enough. Even though I was getting drunk with my mother just last night. Even though, let's face
it, she doesn't know me at all anymore. I don't even know myself.

We eat our sandwiches and dip our feet in the water. I try to
shake off my dark mood, but I can't.

"Anna?" I finally say. "Was my dad ever abusive?"

"No!" She looks shocked, like I've just suggested he may have
been an evil clown or a vampire. "Why would you think such a
thing?" Before she even gets the question out, she's already figured out the answer. "Oh, from Cheyenne, of course."

"She says he used to punch through walls with his bare fists.
She said he once knocked down the bathroom door to get in
where she was hiding from him."

She doesn't say anything for a minute and in the silence I hear the low quacking of ducks. "Well, Lacy . . . that's actually true."

The death march beats again in my head. *Pathetic. Psycho. Little bitch. Waste of time.*

"No," I practically scream at her. She is doing this to me. She is taking my father away from me. I've finally figured out that I am like him and now it turns out he's a monster. Just like Cheyenne said. I put my hands over my ears and begin to sob.

"Lacy, Lacy, you need to calm down and listen. It may be true, and I don't know what you're thinking. But let's talk, okay? Can you calm down and hear me out?"

I sniff. I don't know what she can say. He's a monster and I'm a monster and our rage burns inside us like an awful drug. But I choke back my anger. "Okay," I say, sounding pathetic.

"Okay. It's true that your dad did those things. He told me about them. And I'm sure Cheyenne made herself sound like an innocent little victim. But when he broke down the door to the bathroom, it was because she was trying to kill herself."

"What?" I pull my feet from the water.

"She's done it before, Lacy. I don't know how many times. I don't know if she does it to get attention, or if she really wants to die, but she's attempted suicide several times. On this particular occasion, she had taken a bunch of pain pills, and she called her friend Myrna, then locked herself in the bathroom. So Myrna called your dad, and he came right to the house. But he couldn't get her out of the bathroom to help her, so he knocked down the door."

"He was trying to save her?"

"Yeah." Anna looks at me like I'm a thing made of glass.

"What about the other times? When he punched his hand in the walls."

The ducks flap their wings and rise from the water. "I don't have as neat a story about that, honey. Your mom made him really mad sometimes. He punched through walls. That's how he dealt with anger. It was scary when he did that, but he wasn't hurting anyone but himself." I bite at my fingernail. I guess it does make a certain amount of sense. It's a crazy thing to do, but Cheyenne has a gift for making people crazy. I know that better than anyone.

"Okay," I say.

"Okay?" Anna puts her arm around me.

"Yeah." I snuggle in close to her, I let her hold me. It feels good. But I can't let it feel too good. Tonight she'll be going back to Chico, and I'll be going back to the house with red walls and dead butterflies. The house of dying plants. And I'm starting to forget what Chico was like, and why I didn't want to come to Sacramento in the first place. That's probably what's scaring me most of all.

"How is Cheyenne doing?" Anna asks after a bit.

"I don't know. Okay, I guess. Most days she just lies in bed."

"Oh, Lacy. I wish I could take you home with me." I say nothing. I think that is what I want too, but maybe it's just not my destiny. To live in Chico and be a good little girl, practicing white magic and singing to the fairies. The truth is, the world's a dark place, and it's good to be tough, to be able to fight your way through it. Cheyenne can teach me that. That is, if she doesn't kill herself first.

"It's okay," I finally say. "I've made some good friends here. And Sacramento's okay. There are, like, art walks and festivals and stuff."

"I did talk to your father's lawyer again, after —"

"Oh, really? Let me guess. There's nothing you can do?"

"Lacy, you seem so changed. Are you okay?" I look at Anna. She seems hurt, and maybe a little afraid. I want to tell her. I want to be like my dad, or the girl I used to be, but I still think I am losing myself. I don't like this person I've become. My hands and my feet are so cold, I feel like the walking dead, like a ghost of the happy person I used to be. But I already know there's nothing she can do to help me. She isn't my real mom. Cheyenne is.

"I'm fine," I say lightly. "It's hot. And I'm a little worried about Cheyenne. I just have this bad feeling."

"I understand. She's your mother. But I wish you could disentangle yourself from her, just a little. You seem so wrapped up in her again."

My eyes fill. "I'm trying," I say before the sobs return.

⁂

But she is going to leave. She has to leave. And I am on my way home again. Home to my dark red walls, my dying plants, my fairy-tale dungeon where butterflies lie flat against wax slabs.

When we pull up to the house, I try to coax Mr. Murm from his spot in the bus. But he won't come. I don't know what I've done. Even my cat hates me. I say good-bye to Anna. She hugs me, but we both know something between us has been lost.

Climbing up the stairs to the porch, I get the awful feeling again that Cheyenne has done something to herself. I am going to find her with her wrists slashed, or her head slumped lifeless in the oven. But she's in her bed, painting her fingernails the color of tar.

"How was Anna?" she asks mockingly.

"Fine."

"Cat got your tongue?" I don't know why she has to be mean.

"It was fine," I say again. "We got sandwiches, we went to the river."

"Mmmm, and what kind of sandwiches did you two little vegans get?"

"We're not vegans," I say before I can stop myself. It is the wrong thing to say. Pitting Anna and me together, we versus they, us versus you.

"I'm sorry. Vegetarians," she sneers in a cruel whisper.

"Mom. What do you want me to say?"

"Say what you want to say. 'I want to go live with my precious Anna? Oh, Mommy, please release me so I can be a pure being?' You can pine all you want after your perfect little stepmom. It doesn't matter. You belong to me, heart and soul."

"Fine!" I leave her room and slam the door. In my own room, I pace, like an animal in a cage.

After a while, I go out the window and to Myrna's shop. I need to talk to someone.

CHAPTER SIXTEEN

"She says I belong to her, heart and soul. What do you think that means?"

Myrna brings me a cup of tea. "I'd offer you sugar," she says, "but I seem to have misplaced my sugar bowl."

I fold my hands in my lap. "I'm sorry," I say. "I'll bring it back."

"Keep it." Myrna sits beside me at the monster table. "I know where they sell more."

I reach for the tea and take a small sip. It is hot and good. Myrna watches me, and I lean toward her. "The thing is, I feel like my heart is not my own. I don't even feel it beating. And feel my hands and feet. They're so cold all the time." Myrna reaches out with her own hand. It too feels like ice. I look at her. "What is she doing to us?"

Myrna sighs. "Did your mom ever tell you she and I have been friends since grade school?"

"No," I say. "I can't imagine Cheyenne as a kid."

Myrna laughs, a dry thin laugh, like a cough. "She was a very stoic child. I remember one time some of us kids were hanging out in an empty lot. A boy had found a baby rattlesnake, and he was trying to scare us with it. But your mom, she just reached out her palm. The boy had the snake by its neck so it couldn't bite, but when your mom put her palm out, the snake slithered right onto her hand and stayed there, like it was just waiting to see what would happen next. So then everyone started daring your mom, saying there must be something she was afraid of. She insisted there was nothing. And then this one kid, Joey Riordan, says, 'What about being buried alive?' And do you know what your mom said? She goes, 'Get me a shovel, I'll dig the hole myself.'"

I have to laugh. "That sounds like my mom."

"Of course, it was too hard for her to dig the hole by herself, so we all helped. And eventually, there was this deep hole in the ground, and there was nothing left for your mom to do but climb in. And she did it."

"And they buried her?"

"They did, yes."

I swallow. "How did she get out?"

"Well, it took a while. We left her there. It was a terrible thing to do, but our moms were expecting us for dinner and Joey said it didn't really count unless she was in there for at least an hour. He said he'd come back and get her after dinner. But one thing led to another, and he had to wait until his parents were asleep to sneak out and dig her up."

"Was she okay?"

"I wasn't there, and I asked Joey about it later, but he wouldn't tell me anything. But the next morning, she was there at the bus stop, all clean and showered, her hair braided. Her eyes, though, looked flat . . . almost like bus tokens. Unseeing, you know? I don't think she was ever the same after that."

"That's when she started doing crazy things?" I bite my lip, feeling sorry for her. Not for the Cheyenne I know, but for that little girl at the bus stop. For how she must have felt that day. And for that little girl under the earth. What did she think about? What did she go through?

"It seems like it started right around that time. Her eyes stayed flat like that for years. No depth, no feeling, and she started acting like she couldn't feel anything. I mean, physically, she could, but things the other kids said, or the things her parents made her do, none of it affected her anymore. Like she was a ghost in a human's body. That was when I became interested in the macabre. I wanted to know what your mom knew. When I saw her at the bus stop that day, I felt like I was witnessing a miracle. All night I had dreamt of dirt and coffins, of choking, of dying. But your mom didn't die. She lived. I have no idea how. I've done research since — what she did is impossible, unless there was an air pocket, but even then, it's so unlikely. . . . So maybe she died and came out on the other side. We've been friends ever since, not because we like each other so much, but because I witnessed her death and resurrection, and neither of us would ever see the world the same again."

"Why did you give her all these clothes?" I finger the black rose necklace at my chest. "What do you owe her for?"

Myrna stands up, takes a package of cookies from a high counter, and opens them over the sink. "I love my husband," she says, putting the cookies on a plate. "I've loved him since high school, when his family moved to California from Denmark. By the time we were seniors, I knew I was going to marry him. But there was a senior trip. Lars couldn't go, and I figured, I'll have my whole

life to be tied down. So I had a little fling, and I got pregnant."
Myrna puts the plate of cookies on the table beside me and sits
back down. I imagine it. She would have been only one year older
than me.

"When I got home, I freaked out. I told your mom everything.
I told Lars that I was pregnant too, but I never told him the baby
wasn't his. We decided to get an abortion. We were still young.
But your mom knew. And every once in a while, she reminds me
of that. If she told Lars, it would destroy us. He's my life. So I give
her what she wants. She doesn't ask for much."

"But that's terrible! You're supposed to be her friend. I can't
believe she'd blackmail you."

"Can't you?" A dark look crosses Myrna's face. It is the look of
a girl who has been hurt, a girl who has been stolen from.

"Why is your skin so cold? Why is mine? What did she mean
when she said she owns me, heart and soul?"

Myrna reaches toward me and touches my rose necklace. "She
asked me to make this for you," she says. "It's an old charm. It's
meant to capture your soul."

I feel suddenly sick. I tear the charm from my neck, and the
petals break off, turning papery and crisp like dead leaves. They
fall to the table and I feel more grounded than I have in weeks. "It
occurred to me that it might be a charm. But I thought it was a
good one."

"No," Myrna says.

I shake my head, sad and confused. "Why did you do it?" I ask.

Myrna's eyes fill with tears. "I love my husband," she says.

⟡

It isn't enough. I have removed the necklace, but I'm still cold as stone. I feel empty as the drum of the Tin Woodsman. I remember back to the first night I was here. I drank my mother's tea and it made me sleepy. She asked me to take out the garbage. Shards of glass fell to my chest. I bled. I took my shirt off. And then I fell asleep.

And when I woke up the next morning, it was gone.

"Where is my heart?" I slam through the door of her bedroom. Cheyenne laughs. "Your what?"

"My heart. I know you have it."

"Your heart? Your heart what?" She looks at me coolly.

"My. Heart." I slap at my chest. "You said you own me, heart and soul. I took my soul back. Now I want my heart."

"Oh, Lacy. I didn't mean I have . . . your heart . . . in my possession." She's acting like she's trying not to laugh. "Don't be so literal."

"I haven't felt my heartbeat since I got here. And my hands. Touch them. They're freezing."

"Poor circulation. Your father's side of the family."

"Where is it?" I ask again, looking around her room. Her bathroom. Hadn't she told me never to go in there? I'd never bothered, it was just a bathroom. Now I push through the door. Cheyenne is on me in a minute, holding my arm above my head. She reels me to face her.

"You are crazy," she tells me. "You have always been crazy."

"I'm not crazy. You're the one who's crazy."

"You used to have this imaginary friend. What was her name? Fanny?"

I remember. "So what? All kids have imaginary friends."

"Not like this one. You actually saw her. You would have conversations until late in the night. I'd have to threaten to separate you to get you to shut up."

I remember. The fear of being alone, without Fanny. But she was imaginary. I knew she was imaginary.

Cheyenne drops my hand and it falls to my side. "Go ahead," she says. "Look for whatever it is you're looking for. Your heart."

It strikes me how crazy I must sound. That I think she could take my heart in my sleep without me knowing. Exhausted, I walk out of her bedroom. I need to think.

CHAPTER SEVENTEEN

From my bedroom, I can hear Cheyenne. She is in the kitchen, banging pans like she's trying to beat them to death. Maybe she's pretending they're me. After a bit, she comes into my room.

"I'm sorry we fought," she says. "The truth is, I get a little jealous of your relationship with Anna." She holds a cup out to me, her strange tea. "You must be exhausted and so confused, thinking I've stolen your heart. You've always had a rich imagination. Here, let me tuck you in." I take the tea and place it on my dresser. Cheyenne's right. I am tired. I lie down on the mattress and let her tuck me in, like she maybe used to do once, when I was very young.

"I do worry about you sometimes," she says, stroking my hair. "The things you conjure up in your mind. Do you know, when you were little, you believed in fairies. Not the way most little girls believe in them. You thought they were writing you notes. You thought they were sending you messages." She shakes her head. "My poor girl. Drink some tea. Get some rest. Tomorrow will be better." She leaves the bedroom, closing my door behind her. I can smell the tea from here. Maybe I am crazy. If I'm crazy, I can do whatever I want all day. I can lie in the sun and burn myself to a crisp. I can sing while I'm gardening, laugh when bad things happen. I can stay in bed all day, watch TV, and if I don't feel like swallowing, I'll just let my spit hang from my mouth until I feel like mopping it up.

But I don't think I'm crazy. She does have my heart. I'm going to have to find it. I leave the tea on the dresser, untouched.

⁛

Waiting for Cheyenne to fall asleep, I take the box out from behind my mattress, and take out the things that are in it. A mermaid's eye. An egret's feather. I wish some of their magic could rub off on me. "Where is my heart?" I ask aloud. I put the items back in the box and put the lid back on. About a year ago, I decoupaged the surface of the box with black-and-white photographs from an old magazine. There is a picture of a seagull in flight taking food from a girl's hand. There's one of a chic woman with a smoking gun by her feet on the floor. My favorite photo is one of a little girl and her puppy, but my eyes gloss over that one and land on a picture of a dock. I stare at the dock, and I don't know how I know, but there is an answer for me at the river, I'm sure of it. The mermaid's eye gleams at me in confirmation, and I pocket it.

Finally, Cheyenne falls asleep, and I sneak out. Like with Drake, I go out through the window.

The night is cool. In Chico, the heat sticks around, so day burns into night and it feels like the stars are aflame. But here in Sacramento, the breeze blows in from the delta, and after the sun goes down, the world begins to cool. I head to the river.

At night it looks like a river of blood. Or maybe I'm just being crazy again. I feel like I'm turning into Cheyenne. I need to get my heart back before she takes me over completely.

I kneel in the sand along the shore, and without meaning to, I begin to dig. I dig until I am digging up clams, poor souls who washed in with the current. Horrified, I toss their bodies back into the river, cover the hole with chilled damp sand. And suddenly I know. I know what she's done with it.

CHAPTER EIGHTEEN

There is no moon, dark of the night. A time to cast for beginnings, for fresh starts. The backyard is very dark, aside from the eerie green glow of the pool. Like a cat's eye in the night. The poppy plant looks like it has grown since just yesterday; its blooms are as big as rubies and just as red. It thrives as if it is being fed by a nutrient so powerful it could keep a human being alive, so amazing it could become a symbol for all that is love and desire.

I kneel in the dark earth and pull at the plant. It resists, clinging to the earth, wrapping its thick strong roots like dirty veins around my heart. I will have to pull it apart to make it let go. I stand, about to go to the potting bench for a shovel, when I see her. How long has she been here, out on this dark night, watching me? Her shadow sways, and her mouth opens. Her teeth are like green pearls in the light cast from the pool. She looks like a mermaid or a monster. "What are you doing?" she asks.

"I'm digging it up. It's poison. It's poisoning all the other plants."

"Who are we to turn up our noses at poison?" my mother says. "We are the Fins. We embody poison. Our sharp teeth, remember? Fierce birds with gilded wings?"

"I don't want to be a fierce bird. I want to be who I was before I came here."

"Impossible," my mother says. "That girl wasn't really you."

"It was me. It will be me again."

She yawns. "Lacy, I'm tired. It's late. Can we end this charade? Let me tuck you in. I'll make you some tea." It hits me. I know what her tea is. Poppy pods. Opium. Charmed opium, fed by my own heart.

"I don't ever want any more of your tea."

"Then what the hell do you want?"

"I want my heart back."

Her words come cold and hard as steel. "You can't have it. It's mine now."

I walk toward her. "It's not yours. It doesn't belong to you. I don't belong to you."

"Listen to me." She grabs my arms, and her fingernails dig into my skin. "You are not the one in charge here. I am." She squeezes tighter, and I remember the day she burned me. She held me tight with one hand and, with the other, put her cigarette to my wrist. "No. More. Questions," she had said. I was six. I squeeze my eyes closed and try not to cry. I can't fight Cheyenne. She will win. She always, always wins.

"You're hurting me," I tell her, and I hear a sound like rain. She squeezes tighter and I open my eyes, expecting to see drops falling, to feel them against my skin. But instead of rain I see the flapping wings of a butterfly. It lands on my mother's mouth. Its wings shine green in the night.

"Goddammit," Cheyenne says, releasing me to brush the butterfly from her lips. My arms throb, but I go for the shovel. I reach past her to the potting shed and she grabs my wrist; her fingers burn my skin. "No," she says like a command. But she is *not* the one in charge. I rap hard on her hand with my knuckles and she lets me go. I grab the shovel.

"Lacy!" she shouts as I go back and dig with the steel into the flesh of the poppy plant. "Don't you dare do this to me," my mother growls. She changes tactics. "Please," she says. "It doesn't matter anyway. You can't change who you are." But she's wrong. I can change. I've done it before.

Again I stab at the plant. I can feel it loosening its grasp. Then it releases. I push it to the side and dig in the earth, gently, with my fingers, until they reach something wet. The thing emits a glow through the dark earth; my blood surrounding it glows too, like scattered jewels. I pause for a moment to catch my breath, and then my mother is behind me, her palm against my face, wrestling with my arm. I shove her away hard, afraid that she will crush my heart, and she looks at me, furious.

"You are just like me. Mean enough to hurt your own mother. Cold enough not to care."

"Of course I care. I wouldn't hurt you," I scream.

"Only because you can't. Because I did a binding spell against you."

"It doesn't matter," I say fiercely, her silhouette black against the glow from the pool. "I wouldn't."

Again she grabs at me, but I am stronger now that I have seen it. I strike without thought, pushing her backward, and she topples into the murky pool. When she surfaces, her face is lit up green and gold. The butterfly lands on her wet hair. The gash on her forehead is almost invisible — the plantain tincture worked its magic as I knew it would. And she is beautiful.

"Do you know why I wanted you here?" she asks. "Why I came after you in Chico?" She is shivering, but she continues. "I thought you and I could be amazing together. Don't you see? With our power, we could change the world, you and I."

"I don't think that's why you wanted me," I say.

Her eyes fill. "Sometimes I don't know what I want," she admits. She reaches out her arms. "Please," she says.

But I turn my back to her and gently dig up my heart. It glows in my hand like a great glittering thing. I swallow it whole. It tastes like rosemary and earth.

"I do love you," I whisper. But I know what the butterfly knows. The struggle to leave the cocoon is what strengthens the butterfly's wings so she can fly. I am about to become something beautiful.

⁝

Heat flows outward from deep inside. I feel warmth moving down my arms, my legs, into the tips of my fingers and toes. I feel my heart beat in my chest. With every beat I'm being pumped with a newer sense of compassion, not only for Cheyenne but also for myself. I look at my mother shivering in the pool. Her eyes are dark and dull as stones. She reaches up, touches her head with her fingertips.

"Come on, Mom," I say, reaching out my hand.

Like a child, she looks up at me, she takes my hand, and she doesn't pull me in. She lets me help her out. I go inside for a blanket and wrap it around her, and her shivering begins to slow.

I think of her as a young girl, fearless. The kind of girl who can charm a poisonous snake, or dig her own grave in an empty lot. I wonder again what she thought about, lying for hours in a grave she dug herself. How powerless she must have felt. How utterly alone.

"Lacy?" she says, and her voice is hollow.

"Yes?"

"Do you think I'm unlovable?"

I don't answer at first. I think of the lives she's tried to ruin, the curses and dark spells and the way she's been blackmailing her best friend. That slippery thing in the field that night. Myrna's heart. I'll have to find that field and help Myrna take it back.

But I do love her. Maybe it's a fault of my own, but I do.

"Of course not," I say, and she sighs, leaning her head against my shoulder. I am almost as tall as she is, I notice. I'm not an adult, but between the two of us, I'm the closest we've got. I lead her inside, making sure she doesn't trip over the shovel.

CHAPTER NINETEEN

We sit on the couch, drinking real tea, made from peppermint leaves and purchased at Trader Joe's. She has showered and her hair falls across her shoulders in glossy waves; her kimono falls open, revealing the smooth tan space between her breasts. She looks exhausted. To me, she has never looked prettier.

"Are you sure Anna wants you?" she asks, but I don't think she's being mean. I think she's just making sure.

"I'm sure," I say. I want to tell her that she can visit anytime, but I think it might be best if we don't see each other for a while.

"You know" — she looks down at her fingernails — "I've never cared for Anna. She seems so . . . vanilla."

"She is. That's one of the things I like about her."

"I know. You and I . . . maybe we aren't as alike as I thought."

"I think I'm like my dad," I say. She nods and doesn't comment. She is going to let me have it, this belief.

"Those spells we used to do when I was little. Did we ever do anything to hurt him, or Anna?"

She is silent for a moment. "No," she finally says. "You wouldn't let me. I told you that."

"Did you really do a binding spell on me?"

"Yeah. Right before you got sick. I saw what you did to the frogs, and I was afraid you'd do something to me. I hadn't realized how powerful you were until then. And just so you know, I didn't go against my promise. I didn't use magic on your dad or Anna. But you never said I couldn't use it on you."

The ridiculousness of that loophole. But wait. A binding spell. Right before I got sick. Which means Drake's car accident has to have been a coincidence. I couldn't have hurt with magic if I'd been bound. I still could have done the binding spell. But I couldn't have used magic to hurt anyone.

"Well, can you remove it? I just want to be me. I want to have the power to choose to be good. I want to be good from now on, but I want that to be my choice, Mom."

"Yes," Cheyenne says. "I'll take it off. And yes. You are like your father," she admits. "He must have been proud of you." For a moment it looks like she has softened, like she may even tear up, but her face hardens. It occurs to me that I've never seen my mother cry, except for those choking sobs when she was having her stomach pumped. Maybe that's how she protects herself. Like me with my cutting. Maybe she is afraid of the beautiful feelings inside her.

I reach out for her hand and take it. Her hand is warm, and so is mine. Soon I will let go, though, and I'll fly away.

CHAPTER TWENTY

Crossing the park after school, I see Anna out gardening in the front yard.

"Hey, senior," she calls, seeing me coming. "How was the first day of school?"

I do a little dance as I cross the street, and Mr. Murm comes murming up to my feet. I pick him up and nuzzle my nose into his glossy black fur.

"It was good," I tell her. "My math teacher's really cool. She's going to teach us about the history of the mathematicians. And physics is going to be awesome. And it was nice to see Zach again. He asked me to go see a movie with him Friday night."

Anna reaches out to pet Mr. Murm. "That sounds like fun," she says. "I'm glad to hear school went well."

"I miss Martin and Stacia, though," I say, even though they were just up visiting last week. They had gotten along well with my old Chico friends. It would be so cool if we could all be together. "I wish they went to school here."

"Make it official?" Anna plucks a dandelion from a crack in the sidewalk. I take it and blow, spreading dandelion seeds into the hot Chico air. I know it won't come true, but there's no harm in wishing. Like Anna says, magic exists in the everyday.

For dinner, we have a picnic at Alligator Hole. Tomatoes and basil and thick hunks of mozzarella cheese. I lean back on the beach blanket Anna made, remembering the time we came here with my dad, that day that had wings. And I think of Cheyenne, and I feel a little pull, a little tug. I still love her, and I wish her well, but this is what we've agreed on, and I know it's good. I know she might be back for me one day, the smell of her perfume in the kitchen. But I'm stronger now. And she isn't here now, not even in the deepest recesses of myself. I am purely, majestically, me.

"Look," Anna says. I sit up and she is pointing to a light above Big Chico Creek.

"What is that?"

"I don't know, there're a few of them." The lights flicker in the growing dark.

"Fireflies?" I ask. We don't have fireflies in Chico.

"Maybe they're fairies," Anna says. Her voice is full of wonder. We are learning, together, that anything is possible. My heart fills. We lean against each other and watch as the fireflies or fairies flit and dance in the late summer air.

ACKNOWLEDGMENTS

My most heartfelt thanks to my agent, Molly Ker Hawn. Molly, working with you has been such a magical experience, and I can never thank you enough. Thanks to Jenny Bent at the Bent Agency for recognizing Molly and me as kindred souls and forwarding my manuscript to her. Thank you to Mallory Kass for bringing my book to Scholastic! It has been such a pleasure working with you. Thanks to everyone at Scholastic for all the encouragement. I was always the kid who bought more books from the Scholastic Book catalogs than could be reasonably stacked on my desk at school, and it is such an honor to be an author for this amazing company.

Thanks to my mom, Karin Ireland, my always first and most critical reader. Your insights are invaluable and I am forever grateful. Tina Cooper, Tracy Thompson-Parker, Kathy Katayama, Holly Coady, and Haesoon Maytorena are in my book group. They read an early draft, and loved me and trusted me enough to tell me the truth. I hope they know I appreciate that more than I can say. The same is true for my niece, Kayla Stirling. Thanks to Jennifer Olden and Shane Gallaway for help early on, when the manuscript was a clunky, wingless thing. Erin Azevedo has been enthusiastic and encouraging and reminded me to keep writing when the writing got tough. Maureen Wanket has helped me through every stage of the writing process. Maureen, I hope we're still writing together when OA becomes a genre.

Thank you to my kids, Tyler, Ireland, and Liam. You have truly taught me to see magic in the everyday. Thanks to my dad, Tom Ireland, for being awesome. And thanks to Shane. You inspire me and I love you so.